The Ambassador

The Ambassador

QUEEN OF
INFLUENCE

Patrick W. Andersen

Contents

1

∽

CHAPTER 1

The man kept his conversation businesslike, but Gretchen could sense that the atmosphere practically dripped with sexual tension. He maintained eye contact, rather than letting his gaze drift downward to her Vee-neck as was so often the case with other men. And he kept an arm's length away, rather than concocting a lame excuse to brush up against her in the crowded room.

But Gretchen, who had been doing this for years, detected the telltale signs in his demeanor. The seemingly innocent but ambiguous words peppered throughout his comments, that crept right up to the edge of double entendre without crossing the line. The vague references—reiterated several times in case she had missed it—to being alone here because his wife had a social commitment back home and could not join him for the trip. And, in case the earlier hints had all gone over her head, even a series of comments naming the hotel where he had booked a luxury suite for this event, which, oh dear, he now realized was much too large for a single person. So, while Gretchen might tease him very subtly, she must also maintain a strictly businesslike tone. She raised her wine glass for a slight sip. While the liquid glowed a light amber like a good Chardonnay, her glass actually contained water with food coloring.

The glint from the wine class reflected the late afternoon sunlight from the huge window that stretched across the back wall of the conference room. Outside was a glorious view of a San Diego marina, with lines of grand yachts and smaller sailboats tied up at their berths. Gretchen guessed there was little or no wind outside, as the boats barely swayed and the flags that were in her line of sight mostly hung limp on their poles.

"I am surprised at the number of young people here today," said the man, whose name was Charles Benson. "I was under the impression that the cruise industry attracted mostly elderly people, and that the average age of passengers on most cruise ships is about seventy years or more. In fact, I thought that the name of this particular cruise line, Centennial, was a signal that the minimum age was close to one hundred."

Gretchen smiled at his small joke, but also at the comment itself. This exact point was central in the brand ambassadors' meeting before this cocktail reception, and this man had cued it up as if he were part of the planning team.

"That was true when my generation could not afford such luxuries," she commented as she took another sip from her glass. "But many of us got in on the ground floor of the cryptocurrency market, and we invested well. Later, we got out before the crypto crash and diversified our investments into stocks and bonds, and bought back into crypto when it had bottomed out and started climbing again. We are now in a position to enjoy our success. I am here not only as a cruise passenger, but I am also looking into buying stock in the company."

Charles, whose age Gretchen estimated somewhere in the late fifties, raised his eyebrows in interest. "Cryptocurrency, you say? But wasn't that just a passing fad? Back when I was young, we had pyramid schemes. Wasn't your crypto pretty much the same thing?"

The young woman resisted the urge to roll her eyes. "Crypto is a commodity that can be used like cash. It is not cash. It is a commodity," she explained. But she wanted to pivot the conversation to her preferred topic because cryptocurrency had nothing to do with her objective this afternoon. "So, like any other commodity, the wise investor buys when the price is low and sells when it peaks. Then, when it declines, one waits until it hits bottom and is due to rise again before buying. I am looking at the cruise industry the same way. The price of cruise line shares plummeted during the COVID-19 pandemic. So now is the time to buy. I am not looking to turn an overnight profit on this investment. I will keep these shares for years, and I expect a huge return not only in dividends after the industry recovers, but especially when I sell off the shares in five, ten, or fifteen years when the industry is peaking again and the prices are much higher."

Charles had been sipping his wine enthusiastically while Gretchen spoke, and she noticed that now he did let his gaze drift lower to her Vee-neck. He had even been so crass as to raise up on the balls of his feet as if he were impressed by her economic analysis, though the heightened position obviously gave him a chance to try to look deeper into the Vee. Her jacket matched her slacks in a cranberry shade, red enough to command attention but not so red as to appear flamboyant. She had tastefully avoided showing very much of her ample fleshy cleavage when dressing for this meeting, but the Vee-neck created an illusion that accomplished the task nevertheless.

"Charles, do you follow the market?"

He almost hiccupped into his wine glass, quickly looking up into her eyes again as he tried to reply. "Oh yes. I do dabble a bit in stocks here and there."

"Well, Charles, I earned my undergraduate degree in economics at a business school you have probably heard of. I won't mention names, but it is located in Pennsylvania. I monitor national and international markets and their long-term prospects, and I do not make investment decisions lightly."

Charles appeared to be contemplating her words and thinking how to reply. But at that moment, out of the corner of her eye, Gretchen caught movement across the room. Heidi, one of her colleagues, appeared to be helping an obese elderly man regain his balance after he had stumbled. But Gretchen could see the most likely cause for his "stumble." To prevent himself from falling, he had reached out to her to brace himself. His hand clutched the full cup of Heidi's left breast. After regaining his balance, he removed his hand, and his head was bobbing up and down in what Gretchen assumed were profuse apologies for his clumsiness. None of their other colleagues seemed to have noticed, so Gretchen knew she should act.

Charles Benson seemed to have reached the tipping point anyway, both with his investment decision and his appreciation for the wine. He had raised his hand to signal to a server for a refill of his glass. Gretchen felt she had accomplished her goal with him.

"Charles, forgive me for a moment, but I need to see someone for a quick word. Will you be okay by yourself for a few minutes?"

Gretchen made her way across the room to where her friend and coworker was assuring the man that it was quite all right, that he had just lost his balance. "Hi, is everything okay over here?" Gretchen asked as she reached the pair. "It looked like you were already onboard the ship and we had just hit some rough water that caused you to take a tumble."

Heidi gave a cheerful smile, but her eyes seemed to signal a note of gratitude to her co-worker. "It is okay. Mr. Nichols here was just commenting about a dancer he once saw on the Lido Deck of a luxury ship, and I think he instinctively started to mimic her moves."

Mr. Nichols averted his eyes after glancing briefly at Gretchen. "I guess that was it. I slipped."

Gretchen smiled again as she reached out to lay a hand lightly on the man's right forearm. "Well, perhaps we will all get a chance to dance together in that lounge on the Lido Deck sometime soon." Nodding toward her colleague, she said in a seemingly nonchalant tone, "Mr. Nichols, can I borrow your friend Heidi for a few minutes? The hors d'oeuvres seem to be late, and we need to find out what has happened to them. I don't know about you, but this wine is going to my head, and I need to put something solid in my stomach."

The man's wide face puffed out in a relieved smile. "Quite all right. And I do hope we see each other onboard a cruise ship in the near future. The very near future, in fact."

Gretchen and Heidi navigated through the crowd with their arms linked together, thus subtly marking themselves as off-limits while they made their way across the room. Though none of the cocktail reception's attendees tried to stop the pair to strike up a conversation, many sets of eyes turned to watch them go by. Gretchen and Heidi had dressed in smart business attire, but enough of their feminine charms radiated outward to draw rapt attention not only from the men but many of the women in attendance at the event as well.

When they turned the corner toward the doorway for the kitchen staff, Gretchen halted and swung around to face Heidi. "I am so sorry that man groped you. Are you okay?"

Heidi gave a dismissive shrug. "I have had worse, and by men much younger and more aggressive, who would have been quick to try to follow it up with a more direct attack. In this case, at least, I can be fairly certain that this guy probably wouldn't be able to 'rise to the occasion' if he tried to follow it up later with anything more aggressive than copping a feel." She made an exaggerated display of brushing off the front or her jacket where the man had groped her. "And now we know that he is pretty certain that cruise ship passengers are much younger and prettier nowadays than they used to be."

"Yes, that was the main branding objective," Gretchen nodded in approval. "How about the second objective? Do you think he will buy stock?"

Heidi tilted her head and furrowed her brows slightly, but not enough to crease her makeup. "I am not sure. It sounds like he has a lot of capital, but he is trying to decide between our cruise line and fossil fuels."

Gretchen placed her hand on Heidi's forearm just as she had done with Mr. Nichols a few minutes earlier. "Maybe you can just briefly and casually mention how solar power, wind turbines, and other sustainable energy sources are increasing in popularity?"

"Good idea," Heidi agreed. "How about yourself? How are things going?"

"My guy is a hard one. That is, he is a difficult one," Gretchen added with a grin when she saw Heidi start to giggle. "I researched his assets before we came here, so I know he could easily sink at least a million dollars into the stock if he wanted to. But I think he is going to try to get onto a Centennial ship to find out if there really are a lot of younger passengers. I am going to ask Eric to have the cruise line flag this man's name, so we know if and when he buys tickets. If he does, we may need to book a bunch of us as passengers on the same ship to make him believe he needs to invest."

"Maybe we should send some of our male ambassadors too?" Heidi asked.

"Absolutely. We will want them to ask the wives to dance while you and I keep the men busy. The husbands often make the investments, but the wives tell them what they think would be good. And if the wives have danced with some of our guys, they will tell their husbands what we want them to." Gretchen chuckled. Turning back toward the conference room, she said, "Let's get back to the party."

"Do you think we should check on the hors d'oeuvres like we said we would?"

Gretchen shook her head. "Not necessary. The kitchen staff know what they are doing. I just said that to get you away from Mr. Touchy-Feely."

As the two returned to the conference room, the crowd heard the thump-thump of someone's hand tapping on a live microphone. Turning toward a podium set up on a small riser in the corner, Gretchen saw her boss, Eric Light, the president of the Aurora Marketing Agency, flashing his bright teeth out at the audience. When the voices in the room had died down, Eric cleared his throat.

"I want to thank you all for joining us this afternoon," he said to open his remarks. "I was just commenting that we have so many of the major players in the national economy with us in this room that we could start our own country if we chose to." He stopped while a smattering of polite laughter quickly rose and fell. "But seriously, you are here because you have some of the sharpest minds in the market. You all keep a sharp eye on trends. You all know when to take action. And you all have positioned yourselves over the years to have the wherewithal to act quickly whenever an opportunity might arise. So, I wanted to take just a few minutes of your time before the food arrives to share some news."

Eric took the microphone out of the holder on the podium and held it in front of his chest just below the level of his chin as he stepped out toward the front of the riser, to create a hint of intimacy. "First, let me give you some financial data that you probably know about already. At the close of the stock market this afternoon, the price of Centennial Cruise Line had dropped to seven dollars and forty-two cents a share. And as you probably also know, before the pandemic, Centennial was pushing to just over seventy dollars a share. So, as savvy investors, you are asking yourselves two questions right at this very moment. How low will the price go? And when it rebounds, how high will it go?"

Gretchen glanced around the room. A few of the guests were still chatting quietly among themselves, but most had turned their attention to Eric. She saw a few of them nod their heads slightly when he mentioned the stock price. Although many had been drinking their wine as if their throats were parched just a few moments ago, all glasses were held at chest level now and the servers had retreated to the back of the room.

Eric softened his voice for emphasis. "So, you have almost a ninety-percent decline. Eighty-nine point four percent, if you want to be exact. Now, what was the first thing we all learned when we started venturing into the world of investing? Buy low and sell high. Rinse and repeat. Buy low, sell high. So, Centennial stock is now at a historic low, and that has to have caught your attention or else you would not be here today."

He paused for a moment before continuing. "Let me share with you some information that has not gone public yet." He dramatically held his left up arm in front of his face, pulled his sleeve up and looked at his wristwatch. "It will go public in about twenty minutes when Centennial's press release hits the wires and gets sent almost immediately to the financial news outlets. You are some of the first people in the country to hear this, so please do not tell anyone outside this room that you heard it before it went public. Three months ago, Centennial's bookings for next year's cruise ship sailings were at less than thirty-five percent of capacity. But today, they stand at more than sixty-seven percent, which is on track for sold-out ships by the dates that they set sail next year. And even more interesting," he added, sweeping one hand in an arc to include his full audience, "the demographics have changed dramatically. More singles are booking than ever before, more young people looking for adventure and," he paused for dramatic effect, "looking for love. The kids who used to buy railroad passes to bum around Europe with a backpack have grown up. And they tried land tours but found themselves spending way too much time going in and out of airports, checking in and out of hotels, packing, unpacking, and packing again to move on to the next destination. Instead of traveling from hotel to hotel in the cities they visit, they have learned the advantage of taking their hotel, restaurants, and nightclubs with them from city to city on a cruise ship. We are witnessing a huge shift in the industry, and you all have a chance to get in early. Buy low, as they say."

Eric made a few more remarks, but Gretchen knew he would not talk the topic to death. These people were smart enough to do the math without further coaxing. Even though he had asked them not to share the information outside of the conference room, several had already pulled their cell phones out and started calling and texting. Back at their offices, their assistants would already be checking data and making calculations to text back to their bosses here at the reception. Glancing back to Charles Benson, she saw that he was not even being so subtle. He was speaking heatedly into his phone, and he had a determined look on his face. At one point, he waved his fist up and down as he barked orders into his phone. Gretchen had no doubt that if Mr. Benson were seated in his office in his company headquarters, he would be pounding his desk so hard that his administrative assistant in the reception area outside would hear the thumping of his fist against the mahogany desktop.

"And now, I think the food is here at last," Eric said, motioning as a dozen servers bearing trays of finger food swept around the corner from the kitchen exit and into the conference room. As the guests sampled the hors d'oeuvres and refilled their wine glasses, they chatted among themselves. Many, however, continued texting or talking on their cell phones, indicating to the servers that they would get food and more drink later.

* * *

Later, after the guests had left, Gretchen gathered in the center of the room with Eric, his assistant, Bobbie, and the fifteen of her female colleagues who had worked this event. Now that the workday was over, the women had real wine in their glasses instead of the colored water that they had used during the reception to make the investors believe that the beautiful young women might get tipsy. Now, they looked relaxed but weary as they compared notes and shared stories about how the prospective investors had treated them in conversation. Heidi's groper sounded like the most extreme case of improper behavior, but even the seemingly genteel dialogue offered by some of the other old men left the young women wanting to wash their hands and faces afterward to get rid of the slime.

Eric looked up from the screen of his iPad and waved his arm to catch everyone's attention. "Heads up, ladies. I have got some preliminary results here."

Gretchen and her colleagues stopped speaking immediately and turned attentively toward their boss.

"Centennial's president sent me an encrypted text message. He has received serious contacts from several of our guests this afternoon. Of course, he won't have firm figures until the investors actually place their orders. But the discussions so far indicate that, collectively, several of our guests are buying at least twenty million dollars' worth of stock when the market opens." Eric paused for a moment. "Who can tell me what the immediate impact of that will be?"

Gretchen raised her hand but did not wait for him to call on her. "Other large investors will sense the momentum and will rush to buy shares before the price rises too high. Then thousands of small investors will see the sudden movement and try to jump onboard, driving the price even higher. And all that interest in the cruise industry will convince millions of vacationers that it must be safe again to get onboard a ship with thousands of other passengers, or else why would smart investors put in so much money? And if they think the ships will be filled with young, attractive singles looking for dates, a lot of elderly passengers will be getting onboard and flashing cash. Lots of it."

Eric beamed. "Exactly! Today we started an avalanche. Congratulations, ladies, you have again had a smashing success!"

The women waved their hands together and apart to motion as if they were applauding, but no one actually clapped because they each held a glass of wine in one hand. Several turned and nodded at their neighbors, but all kept silent as Eric prepared to continue.

"So, as I told you at our meeting before the reception, our agency will get a large bonus if all that money comes into Centennial as a result of our work here today. And that means that each of you will be receiving a substantial something extra in your pay envelopes. Again, congratulations on a job well done," he said, raising his glass toward them all.

Eric shifted his weight from one foot to the other as he also shifted the tone of his voice.

"But that is past us now, and we need to prepare for our next job," he began. After swiping his index finger across the screen of his iPad, he stopped to read for a moment as he held his forefinger aloft, pointing toward the ceiling. Gretchen took advantage of the opportunity for a long, deep sip of her wine, relishing the glow it spread through her chest.

"We are flying back to San Francisco on Sunday morning. I think you have all more than earned a Saturday of free time here in San Diego. On Wednesday, we will attend a public forum on fossil fuels, sponsored by our next client. Back at the hotel, I have folders for each of you with the primary objectives for rebranding our sponsor's company image. I will give them to you to start studying on Sunday when we get to the airport, so that you don't have to read the boring in-flight magazines they offer on the plane."

Heidi stirred and raised her hand. "Which side are we supporting on this assignment? I just spent an hour convincing an investor here that he should dump fossil fuels so he could buy Centennial Cruise Line stock instead. I told him renewable energy sources were on the upswing and fossil fuels were going to go down the tubes."

Eric shrugged but continued smiling. "You will be on the opposite side next week, but don't worry. You don't have to argue in favor of polluting the environment. You will just be making it sound like our sponsor, which is a major oil company, needs more time to further develop some exciting and innovative renewable energy sources while it winds down its oil drilling."

Heidi raised her hand again and asked a follow-up. "But are they really winding down their oil drilling?"

Eric shrugged again, laughing this time. "Who knows? I didn't ask."

2

CHAPTER 2

Gretchen had already put lotion on all the areas that she could reach, so she turned to the newest member of the team to ask for a hand. "Candace, can you put sunscreen on my back for me?" Four of the ambassadors had spread large beach towels on the prow of a large motorboat that was now anchored in the bay, and they were sitting on the towels as they watched windsurfers glide across the water on their boards.

"Please, you can just call me Candy," the young buxom blonde responded. She looked at the plastic container before squeezing the lotion onto her palm. "The SPF on this sunscreen is so high that you won't get any tan at all. Why do you even bother laying out in the sun?"

Melanie, who shared Gretchen's olive complexion and glossy black shade of hair, turned her head toward them. "Candace, or Candy if you prefer, our professional life depends on our brains and our beauty. As long as we don't get hung up on drugs or alcohol or toxic relationships, we will probably keep our brains sharp for the rest of our lives. But our beauty? Maybe twenty years. Thirty at the most, and even then, you would be only hosting events as the elderly matron, not the sweet young thing. But if you ruin your skin with too much sun, then you are cutting your career time in half. You might not even get ten years. So, you have to decide what's important to you, a tan that will stay with you for a few weeks, or skin quality that will last for a longer career."

Gretchen turned her face just a bit toward the younger woman massaging lotion onto her back. "Why do you think we wear these big floppy hats? It is not for fashion, though you may have noticed that a lot of the local women here wear them too. It is to keep the sun off of our faces. Your skin will get damaged and wrinkled if you get careless. And how much work as a model and brand ambassador do you think you will get if your face looks crabby?"

Candy finished rubbing the sunscreen between Gretchen's shoulder blades. "I think you are all being a bit paranoid," she muttered.

Just then, a chorus of hoots and howls rang out from another motorboat that was passing nearby on the bay. A half dozen bare-chested young men in swimsuits on the boat waved and whistled. "Hey, babe, ya wanna come take a ride?" called out one of them. His friends all hollered similar invitations, though in cruder language.

Candy grinned. "See what I mean? They don't seem to think we are losing it."

Stephanie, the fourth woman in their party, tried to put a note of patience into the tone of her voice but did not quite succeed. "Candy, ignore those idiots. If you so much as smile or wave at them, they will think that means we all want to talk to them. And if those idiots come pester us because you encouraged them, I personally will hold your head under the water until you stop thrashing and your body goes limp."

Candy gave a loud harrumph. "You guys are no fun at all."

After the boatload of yahoos had gone far enough away that the women could no longer hear them, Melanie asked, "Is anyone going dancing tonight?"

Stephanie propped herself up on one elbow. "The last time I went dancing in San Diego, the club was full of guys just like the ones on that boat. It got to the point that I didn't even want to stand up from my table for fear that I would attract attention or give the impression I wanted to find a dance partner."

Gretchen called out from under her hat. "Yeah, they all just want to stick their hands where they aren't supposed to go in a public place, hoping that later on they'll get to carve another notch in their bedpost."

Melanie laughed at them. "Oh, come on. It is just dancing. They can't drag you out of the club and into their bedroom if you don't want to go."

Stephanie's voice sounded tired. "I know, but we have a plane to catch in the morning. I think I will just have a few drinks at the hotel bar. Maybe they will have live music there too. Gretchen, would you like to join me?"

Gretchen still would not lift the big floppy hat off of her face. "Sounds like a plan."

3

∾

CHAPTER 3

Eric, Bobbie, and the sixteen ambassadors filled the first-class seats. As a result, the face of every man boarding the plane lit up like a high-beam headlight when he saw the beauties facing toward the front of the cabin. As always, the sixteen women had dressed tastefully, but today they wore traveling attire, not elegant business or evening fashions. Most wore short skirts that revealed long, smooth legs. And, owing to the fact that they had just come in from the warm San Diego weather, the straps of their tops went over bare shoulders. They would have easy access to sweaters or light jackets in their bags if cool weather greeted them in San Francisco. The temperature in San Francisco seldom rose above sweater weather, so they always carried an extra layer of clothing in their bags.

As the passengers in the coach seats toted their carry-on luggage up the aisle toward the back of the plane, Gretchen avoided making eye contact with most of them, especially the men. Over the years, she had learned that many of the passengers seemed to instinctively resent those seated in first class. And the men who made eye contact with one of the attractive brand ambassadors might try to make passing conversation or even stop to ask for a phone number. Such chance meetings seldom if ever turned out well, but getting out of such a conversation, once started, could turn awkward or even ugly. Unless she happened to see a current or prospective client in the aisle, she usually preferred to avoid the possibility

15

of even hinting that she would welcome any attention. Better to avoid messy entanglements before they started.

While the boarding continued, Gretchen opened the folder Eric had given her with the background information for this next week's assignment. Having argued for both sides of the fossil fuel debate for various clients that had hired their agency over the years, Gretchen already understood the issue well. But she needed to find out if the current client was building an argument based on new data from new research or just giving a new interpretation of old data to rebrand the client's public image.

So, while her colleagues chatted among themselves or made last-minute calls on their cell phones before the flight attendants called for all electronic devices to be turned off, Gretchen opened her fossil fuels folder. The executive summary gave a one-paragraph overview of the brand objective, followed by a short list of bulleted items for the primary talking points. Gretchen found nothing startling in the summary, and idly turned to the tables of data that could be used to support the talking points. The numbers followed a predictable pattern that resembled old research, and the pie charts made the thesis statement appear to be a reasonable conclusion. By the time the flight attendant started giving the safety presentation on the locations of the emergency exits and how to fasten seatbelts, Gretchen had consumed the contents of the folder and put it back in her bag.

When the plane reached its cruising altitude, the cockpit door opened and the captain walked out to confer with the chief attendant, closing the door behind himself. The attendant nodded her head toward the passengers, and the captain stepped out to the front of the aisle and smiled.

"My crew told me that we had a very distinguished group of business-women flying with us today. I just wanted to thank you for choosing our airline. We know you have plenty of other carriers to choose from, so we are grateful to have you with us today." The captain looked intently at each of the women in turn, though Gretchen noted that he did not seem to notice Eric and Bobbie.

After he returned to the cockpit, Candy turned to Gretchen and remarked, "That was nice of him, wasn't it? The airline really wants our business. Maybe we should set up a business account with them."

Gretchen leaned forward to speak quietly into Candy's ear. "Babe, that was just the captain coming out to look at all the pretty girls. The flight attendant makes that speech about how grateful they are that we chose to fly with them. On every single flight, on every single airline, the flight attendant makes that speech just before we land at our destination. The captain just wanted to take a look at all of us. Don't be surprised if he slips you his business card when you are getting off the plane in San Francisco and tells you to call him anytime."

"Ooh, that would be exciting, wouldn't it?" Candy's eyes opened wide at the thought. "I have heard that airline pilots make a lot of money."

Gretchen patted Candy's shoulder sympathetically. "Babe, you have heard the expression about the sailor who has a different girlfriend in every port?"

Candy giggled. "I didn't say I want to marry him. I just want him to spend a lot of money on me." Candy started to turn around in her seat but arched her back suddenly. "Ow!"

"What's wrong? Did you hurt yourself?"

"Oh, it is nothing, really. I just sunburned my cheeks yesterday on that boat."

Gretchen leaned forward to get a better look at Candy's face. "They don't look burned."

Candy's expression remained deadpan. "Not those cheeks."

4

∽

CHAPTER 4

The cab driver carried her suitcase and garment bag to her front door, and Gretchen gave him a generous tip in cash after having paid the fare by credit card. While she needed the credit card receipt for her business expense records, she did not trust the taxi companies to give their drivers the full amounts of their tips from credit card charges. So, she always tipped in cash.

After turning on the light inside the entrance, she found the living room looking exactly as she had left it. No muss, no dust, no clutter—everything in its place. She glanced at the answering machine and saw no flashing light, no messages. The mail slot on the door contained several envelopes offering her deals on financial services and real estate, and several appeals from charities. But no personal letters.

Years earlier, when she first bought and moved into this condominium, she hired a decorator to coordinate the furniture styles, wall colors and accessories. A few framed paintings hung on the walls. One was a landscape; another was a colorful picture of a bowl of fruit. None included people, and she did not display photos of friends or family anywhere in the house.

After unpacking her bags, and kicking off her walking shoes, Gretchen poured herself a full glass of red wine to unwind. Instead of her usual Cabernet, she chose a Zinfandel because she craved something sweet. She

18

opened her laptop computer and put her feet up on the coffee table in the living room, preparing to settle in for a quiet evening.

First, the email. She read through a list of subject headings that looked like they could have easily gone into the Spam folder. She did not bother to open any of them but moved all of them into the trash. Next, she opened her social media accounts. She found some contacts from lonely old men fawning over her posted pictures, and several more from users promoting their products or services. A couple of women had texted her asking advice on how to become a brand ambassador like her. Nothing personal.

Closing the laptop, Gretchen reached for the remote and turned on the television. On a channel that featured vintage films that probably did not cost much to the TV station, she found an old movie about a woman being courted by a handsome young suitor. She considered much of the dialogue too schmaltzy to take seriously, but the scenery captivated her. She took a long sip of her wine and laid back against the sofa cushion.

Hours later, Gretchen awoke and saw that a televangelist's show now filled the TV screen. The clock read three-fifteen in the morning. Gretchen turned off the TV, rinsed her wine glass at the kitchen sink, and undressed for bed.

5

CHAPTER 5

The office hummed with the usual background noise—a desktop printer rolling out a document, a phone ringing, a few of the brand ambassadors chatting at a third model's desk. After setting down her purse on her own desk in her cubicle next to the window, Gretchen walked to the coffee machine and poured herself a cup. Black. No sugar, no cream, nothing that might add unnecessary calories or animal fat to her daily intake. Waving greetings to those of her colleagues who happened to notice her, Gretchen sat at her desk and booted up her computer.

Opening her encrypted text messaging program, Gretchen found sixty-two unread messages from her contacts. Scrolling through the list, none had come from anyone important. Just her usual "marks." She opened the Greetings document in her word processing software. The first line on the document read, "Good morning. How was your night?" Gretchen highlighted that message and pressed Command-C on her iMac to copy it. Then she gave a command to send blind-copy replies to all the people on this distribution list. She pressed Command-V to paste the greeting into the Reply text message field and then clicked the Send button. She did not bother to open more than a few dozen of the messages the contacts had sent her.

Then she highlighted and copied the second greeting on her word processing document. "My night was good. I hope you have eaten." Only thirty-seven of the contacts had responded to her earlier greeting, so she opened only those. Before pasting in the copied response, she would glance at each to make sure they had not said anything more complex than, "Good, and how was yours?"

Finally, she selected a recent photograph of herself posing in a bikini. The bikini did not cover much of her body, and she had posed seductively yet tastefully, not flaunting any flesh unnecessarily. She attached a caption saying, "This is from my photo shoot yesterday. I thought you would like it." This time, she did not open the text threads of just those who had responded this morning. She gave a command to send the photo and text to each of the one hundred thousand contacts on her list of marks. After clicking the Send button, Gretchen let her shoulders slump for a moment before picking up her cup to go get more coffee.

Shuffling through the small stack of envelopes in her In tray, Gretchen set the junk mail on the corner of her desk above the trash can and put the two envelopes that had been addressed to her by hand on the center of the desk. Opening the first, she found a printed sales letter urging her to buy real estate while the market remained favorable. She tossed the paper toward the trash can, accidentally knocking several envelopes in the junk pile into the can as well. Gretchen did not bother to retrieve them.

The second hand-addressed envelope yielded a more hopeful result. Though the letter inside was typed and laser-printed, the signature was in original ink. A former client of the Aurora Marketing Agency was saying he had been particularly impressed by Gretchen on a project the brand ambassadors had done for his company and wanted to know if she would be willing to take on an independent project for him, without involving her employer.

Gretchen picked up the letter and walked to the door of the private office in the corner. Looking in the open door, she saw Eric speaking to a client's image on his desktop computer. Reaching to extend his hand outside the range of the camera, he waved Gretchen into his office to sit on the guest chair in front of his desk.

"Yes, Mrs. Johnson, my ladies will wear only fashions from your line at the event. I will have my assistant Bobbie get in touch with you to get a list of the items you especially want to promote. I would suggest a range of items from affordable to high-end and all price ranges in between, so as to attract more people."

Finishing up the call, Eric turned to Gretchen expectantly.

Gretchen held up the letter. "Do you remember Mark Fischer from the horse racetrack account?"

Eric nodded. "He paid his bills on time. I don't recall that the campaign was especially noteworthy. He just wanted a bunch of pretty faces at the meeting. I hope none of those people there had connections to the mob. We don't need that kind of entanglement."

Gretchen scanned the letter again before looking up. "He is asking if I want to do an indie project for him, without involving the agency. I don't know this guy except for our job for his racetrack, and I wanted to make sure he wasn't setting a trap before responding. What do you think?"

"Close the door for a moment," he said. After she had done so and seated herself again, Eric leaned forward as if to speak in confidence. "Gretchen, babe, as far as I know, the guy is clean. I didn't get any phone calls or messages from anyone demanding hush money, and nobody made any unusual contacts with me. Usually, if someone is trying to muscle me, I am aware of it fairly quickly."

"So, you think he might be safe?"

"Probably. And look, if you want to do an indie job for this guy, that's okay with me. You deserve it. But if it looks like it is going to turn into a major job needing more people, try to steer him back to me."

"You got it, boss."

6

CHAPTER 6

The office building stood 23 stories high with three large statues at the top. When this building was constructed, those statues probably looked down on most of the surrounding structures. But no more. Other office towers loomed much higher, but this edifice on the corner marked a border of several neighborhoods. Still, the three statues had long been nicknamed The Corporate Goddesses because they looked down upon the heart of the city's business district. Across the street at ground level was another famous sculpture that inadvertently complemented the Goddesses' mission, a giant slab of black granite popularly known as the Banker's Heart, symbolic of the financial district in which it stood. While the city was home to some of the corporate giants of the nation, the locals kept a sense of humor about it and named the landmarks accordingly. A short one-block stroll in the opposite direction to the north would take one into the heart of Chinatown, and a few blocks beyond was the historic North Beach, long the Italian stronghold in the city. As Gretchen stood facing the building, she realized that one of her wealthiest clients conducted business just three blocks up on Nob Hill to her left. Though the city housed many of her clients—both through the agency and on her private list—Gretchen did not relish coming into the city. For one thing, just parking her car could cost as much as a gourmet meal at a fine restaurant.

When the elevator door opened, Gretchen stepped out to the reception desk and asked for Mark Fischer. After calling to announce her arrival, the receptionist escorted Gretchen to a waiting room.

"Ms. Vandella, thank you for coming in," said Mark Fletcher from a doorway into a long hallway.

"Please, call me Gretchen." She rose from the cushioned chair and smoothed her skirt. Not knowing what sort of marketing project the man might be proposing today, she had dressed in business attire. Today's outfit was less severe than what she wore at the San Diego conference, however; rather than the Vee-neck jacket and matching pants, she wore a gray skirt and striped blouse. She left the top two buttons undone, revealing just the beginnings of the swelling of her breasts, under an unbuttoned blazer. She carried a very thin briefcase made of soft, pliable leather as she followed him to an office at the end of the hall. She took a seat in front of the desk; looking around the room, she saw absolutely nothing personal in the decorations. "Mr. Fischer, does your company occupy this entire floor?"

"Just Mark," he smiled. "No, these offices rent out by the day. I mostly work remotely out of my own home, but sometimes I need to hold multiple meetings in the city. So, I often rent an office here because it is centrally located."

Gretchen opened her case and took out a notebook. "If you have several meetings scheduled today, then we should get right down to business. What sort of venture are you planning, and how can I help?"

Mark held his palms up as if to signal a halt. "No, this is the only meeting I have scheduled today. We can take all day if we need to."

"You rented this office today just to speak to me? I am honored." Risking a bit of femininity, she batted her eyelashes as if in modesty.

If Mark noticed the trick with the eyelashes, he did not let on. "Gretchen, this could be very important. I saw how you and your colleagues worked the room during my reception for the racetrack, but I took special note of you. I would like to learn more about you before we get into specifics about my project. When I hired Eric's agency, he was a bit vague about what you and your coworkers actually do. I just saw the results. The people who needed to be convinced, were convinced. It was a good day for my business."

It would have been easier to decide how to proceed, Gretchen thought, if this were Mark's own office. His personal choice of décor—colors, furniture style, pictures on the wall, perhaps family pictures on his desk, the presence or absence of clutter—would give her a better feel for how to read him, how to relate, how to persuade him to the desired viewpoint. Lacking such guideposts, she would have to just feel her way forward, adapting her approach if it became necessary.

"Mark, as you know, the agency does marketing. That word means different things to different people," she said. "Some think marketing is sending brochures by direct mail; others think it involves advertising in publications or on TV. And then there are the billboards.

"My colleagues and I focus more on branding. Your brand is the public's perception of you and your business. If it is done well, maybe people will think of your brand at just the sight of your logo. Some companies focus their brand on how they want customers to think of themselves. Young and smart customers, beautiful people who listen closely to billionaire executives dressed in jeans and turtlenecks, ahead of the field when it comes to being cool."

Gretchen stopped for a moment, distracted by movement on the hill outside the window behind Mark. A cable car was climbing the street past Chinatown toward Nob Hill. Talk about a brand logo! This town had several easily recognizable symbols that triggered recognition almost instantly—cable cars, the Transamerica Pyramid, and of course the Golden Gate Bridge. Any marketer worth her salt did not have to use a thousand words; she had images that would do the work.

Mark folded his hands behind his head as he stretched for a moment. "So, all I have to do is hire you and I will be as famous as one of those huge corporations, eh?"

Gretchen smiled as she shook her head. "Their branding campaigns have been decades in the making and cost many, many millions of dollars. What you saw at your event for the racetrack took a very focused, intense campaign by my colleagues and me. We studied your company's image, determined what we needed to emphasize to the audience you were after on that occasion. Then the men and women of our team drilled ourselves on the objectives—first the primary goal, and then the second, third and fourth outcomes we hoped for We went into that meeting of yours with one objective but a variety of methods to achieve it, to steer every conversation toward your brand, to turn every thought toward identifying with the goals of your campaign.

"That's why, in the industry, they call us brand ambassadors."

Mark's eyebrows rose in twin arches, and he nodded comprehension for what she had said. He glanced at his watch, making a point of hiking his shirt sleeve to look at the dial. "You have given me a good overview. Did you have plans for lunch? If not, could I interest you in a bite?" She nodded assent without a moment's hesitation. Conversations over meals always had better chances of success.

Exiting the elevator and stepping onto California Street, they walked one block up the hill to Grant Avenue. They turned right at Old St. Mary's, a church that dated back almost to the days of the Gold Rush. Mark led them to the door of an old restaurant.

An elderly Chinese man led them to a private booth, where he pulled open a curtain to allow them to sit at the table inside. After bringing them tea and menus, he closed the curtain to shield them from view.

"I have never seen that before," Gretchen commented, gesturing toward the curtain.

"And you will probably never see it again," Mark said wistfully. "This is one of the last vestiges of a world that is disappearing. This restaurant was built a hundred years ago, but its days are numbered. The pandemic nearly destroyed hospitality businesses like hotels and restaurants."

Mark raised his tiny teacup and held it out in a toast. "Good fortune to you." They clinked their cups together and each took a small sip. "I hope you enjoy seafood. They serve it very fresh here."

Gretchen smiled. "I saw the live fish swimming in the tanks as we walked in."

"If you don't mind, I will order tofu dishes and vegetables rather than rice, chow mein or chow fun. I am trying to avoid carbohydrates."

"That is fine. I prefer to avoid those things too, or else I have to put in extra time at the gym to work it off," she commented. She already spent an hour working out a minimum of five mornings each week. Any more could complicate her schedule.

The conversation proceeded smoothly and without any pressure regarding business. Gretchen learned that Mark had grown up in the Midwest, the only child of a factory foreman and housewife. After leaving home and taking a job as a stable hand at a horse farm in Kentucky, he had learned not only about the care and nurturing of horses but also about the regimen necessary to prepare them for racing. From there, it was a relatively rapid rise to management. And then "good fortune" had come indeed. The horse farm raised several high-stakes winners, and Mark received enough money to invest in the racetrack here in Northern California. Over the next several years, he bought out smaller investors and increased his holding to more than fifty percent.

Gretchen, in turn, let him know that though she was born and raised in Southern California, she had moved to San Francisco to enter the modeling business. While living in Anaheim and commuting to work in Hollywood, she happened to meet Eric Light on a photo shoot for one of his clients. He asked if she would be interested in becoming a brand ambassador, combining her modeling skills with her intellect and influencing the spending habits of millions of consumers. She leapt at the chance.

But though she told part of her personal story, she kept most personal details private. She did not want to share the parts of her past that caused the pain and anger that still drove her so hard to this day. The pain had probably given her the drive to succeed and had put her in the position she was in, even put her at this restaurant with him now. But he did not need to know any of that. Some things needed to remain private.

After lunch, Mark paid the bill and the two of them walked back down the hill to the office building. Taking their seats in his office again, Mark put on his business face again.

"Gretchen, you are wondering why I invited you here today. Trust me—I am not being secretive. I wanted to get to know a bit more about you. I am not just hiring a marketing firm, or a branding ambassador, as you call yourself. If things go the way I hope, this will be much bigger than that."

She felt she needed to put on her business face too. "Mr. Fischer, I mean Mark, I am confident that I could help you with whatever your project may be." She reached into her case and began to pull out some paper. "I have a list of past clients and my academic credentials."

"I don't need to see those things," Mark interjected quickly, holding his palm outward as if to push the papers away. "I already have that information, and more. I needed to hear you speak one-on-one, see how you interact when it is not all business. I have a good feel, so I want to tell you a little bit more and see what you think."

Gretchen leaned forward in her seat. The past few hours had led up to this moment. This was what she came here for.

"Through hard work but also a lot of just plain dumb luck, I have made a lot of money. With the investments I have made, I am reasonably confident I can live comfortably for quite some time. I could jump into the race to be the richest bastard in the very large league of rich bastards. Or I could just retire and spend my time going to parties with rich bastards and rich bitches. As you can imagine, I have met quite a few people like that."

Gretchen laughed. "Yes. I think I have come into contact with a large number of them while representing our clients."

Mark nodded with a grin. "Yes, so you will understand why I am not particularly interested in spending the rest of my days trying to be just like those people. Of course, I still need to work with them, but I want to do something different. That's what I wanted to talk to you about."

"You want me to run interference for you? Do the glad-handing and small talk with them at cocktail receptions so you don't have to?" Gretchen offered.

"In a way, but there's more to it." Mark turned in his chair and glanced out the window, but not looking at anything in particular. "When you drove into the city this morning, did you see people on the sidewalk?"

Gretchen shrugged. "Of course. I probably passed hundreds of pedestrians."

"No," he stopped her. "I mean on the sidewalks. Sitting there with all their worldly possessions. Depending on which streets you were driving on, you might have seen them living in tents on the sidewalk. If you walk a few blocks from here, you will see people sleeping in their socks in doorways just off the sidewalk. They sleep in the doorways to avoid getting stepped on by passersby."

Gretchen held up her hand for him to stop. She stood up and walked behind her chair, gazing blindly at the drab office wall. She swiveled her head sideways to look at Mark over her shoulder, and then turned back to the office wall. She raised her hands to the sides of her head but, realizing that she might be mussing her hair, smoothed the locks down and returned to stand in front of her chair.

"Let me get this straight. You want to take on homelessness?"

Mark grinned. "I said it was going to be big."

She sat down, leaned forward, and put her hands on the edge of his desk as if she were going to push it into his gut. Looking straight into his eyes, she said, "Mark, if I just wanted to take your money, I would say, 'Golly, what a wonderful idea. When can I start?' But I can't do that. I have to be honest. The federal government has tried for decades but can't solve homelessness. The state government has been trying just as long but has not been able to solve homelessness. The government of the city we are sitting in here has spent hundreds of millions of dollars on solving homelessness. And as you just pointed out, despite all that money, there are people out sleeping on the sidewalk even as we speak, at this very moment."

Gretchen put her hands on the armrests of her chair and sat up straight. "I have got to tell you, it sounds very idealistic and all, but it would probably be a huge waste of your money."

Mark gazed at her with a noncommittal expression, his fingers laced together as he folded his hands together on the desk in front of him. Gretchen could not read his eyes. His lips were just horizontal lines, forming neither a smile nor frown. His breathing remained steady.

Finally, he stirred.

"You may have wondered why I asked you here today. After all, if I was just after some help on marketing, why wouldn't I consult with Eric, the head of your agency? Or, if I just wanted one of the so-called ambassadors, why you? More than a dozen of you worked the room at my reception for the racetrack. It is not like you have cornered the market on beauty in a crowd or gorgeous models like that, and all of you handled yourselves with poise and intelligence. Why you?"

He unfolded his hands and raised them to support his chin, and he leaned forward with his elbows on the desk.

"I know you do a great deal of research on each of your clients before you ever meet them," he said. "Well, I have done some research too. I know a lot about you. I know a lot about each one of your coworkers at the agency, and I know a lot about Eric too."

Mark sighed audibly. "It takes a lot of balls to call bullshit on a potential client who might represent a lot of income for you." He looked directly into her eyes. "And out of every single employee at your agency, I had a feeling that you would be the only one who had the balls to say my idea was bullshit. Thank you for proving me right."

He straightened up the loose items on the desk and pushed his chair back as if to stand. "I would like to go out to the reception area to get a cup of coffee. Would you like to walk with me?"

Gretchen lifted her briefcase and slung the strap of her purse over her shoulder.

"No, you can leave those things behind. We will be back in a minute or two. Unless you want to leave before even hearing my proposal?"

Confused, she set her bag and case down again and followed him out to the reception area. After he poured them each a cup, she noted that he too did not take cream or sugar. She had read medical research that black coffee did have some benefits, but the popular additives most people used negated them. They lifted their cups gingerly and walked back down the hall to the office to resume their discussion.

"Okay, so let's talk a bit of history," Mark said. "If you try to find out when the word homelessness became part of our everyday language, you won't find much mention of it before the early 1980s. That's when this philosophy took hold of the nation, saying that if you gave more money to the people at the top, it would trickle down to the middle and lower classes, and we would all be prosperous and happy. So that's what we did."

Now he leaned forward again. "But it didn't trickle down. People in the lower classes lost their jobs as the money dried up. They couldn't pay their bills. A lot of them started taking jobs for less pay, creating competition among the poor to see who could sink to the lowest level. becoming the cheapest employees. The ones who won the competition could barely pay their bills, but those who lost that competition got kicked out of their homes."

Gretchen made a motion like she was throwing up her hands. "So, what are you going to do? That has been happening for more than forty years."

Mark's expression and tone made it sound obvious. "Put them to work."

7

CHAPTER 7

The Monday morning staff meeting started promptly at nine o'clock. Thirty ambassadors—twenty women, ten men—sat on cushioned chairs with hard, plastic armrests. Eric stood at the front of the room, next to an erasable whiteboard, and Bobbie sat at a desk to the side with two stacks of folders. The ambassadors all had iPads on their laps, ready to take notes.

The windows on the left side of this meeting room faced east, so sunlight slanted in from that direction. The vertical blinds cast shadows across half the ambassadors as they waited for Eric to begin the meeting.

"We have three items this week," he began. "As you already know, tomorrow on Tuesday I have scheduled five of you to do a photo shoot for a motorcycle company. Greg, Nick and Ron will go, as well as Cheryl and Rosie."

"How do they want us dressed?" Nick asked.

"Leather jackets and blue jeans on the men, bikinis on the women."

"Eric," Cheryl called out, "nobody's going to believe that we ride motorcycles dressed in bikinis. Why can't Rosie and I wear leathers and jeans too?"

Eric gave her a look like she was a child. "Cheryl, no one is going to give a thought to whether you and Rosie are riding. They are going to be looking at *you*. We are hoping that they will also at least glance at the motorcycles and even take note of the company name. But don't tell the company reps that when you meet them at the shoot."

Ron spoke up. "So, what are we guys, chopped liver?"

Eric laughed. "No, I *like* chopped liver. You, I'm not so sure about." He smiled at Ron to make sure he realized it was said in jest.

"On Thursday," he continued, "it is all hands on deck. We are shooting a video at a new conference center in San Jose. High-tech facilities, plus a restaurant and three bars onsite. Smart casual clothes for everyone. Women, show a bit of skin but not too much. Men, it is smart casual, not just casual. Slacks, dress shirts and jackets. High-end materials only, please."

Gretchen raised her hand. "Will we have any speaking parts in this video? Do we have to study their brand highlights?"

Eric shook his head. "No speaking parts. Everybody just has to look pretty. One of their executives wants to do the voice-over."

He paused while the ambassadors all typed in notes on their tablets.

"Friday will require study. A data mining and trading company wants to attract new investors. I need a dozen of you to attend meetings of elderly investors to coax them into sinking money into this fund. Do any of you want to volunteer, or should I make assignments based on who is free?"

Heidi raised her hand. "Why elderly?"

"Because our client thinks elderly investors are more likely to buy into the marketing line that someone in their management team came up with." Eric held up an information sheet and squinted at the text. "They generate profits by using their exclusive monster data mining system, and they protect their money with a lockbox made of iron and steel."

The room erupted in laughter.

Heidi waved her arm back and forth above her head. "No, please, boss. Tell me that's not their pitch."

Eric held his palms up to his sides as if asking, would I kid you?

Nick held a forefinger in the air. "Wait, have they printed any company literature using that terminology?"

Eric shook his head. "Nothing yet. They are waiting for us."

"Then our first assignment is to come up with a more sensible sales pitch. We are already getting close to a federal offense by targeting the elderly. If we use comic book slogans and treat them like children, FBI agents will be knocking on our doors," Nick added.

Ron laughed. "Aren't you being a bit melodramatic?"

Nick did not smile. "Financial Elder Abuse, a federal crime. We have to proceed very carefully here."

The room buzzed with conversation, but Eric punctuated the discussion with a sharp clap of his hands. "Excellent observation. Nick, I want you to head up a team to come up with a new branding proposal for us to present to the client by Wednesday. We need to get them results but protect ourselves at the same time."

Heidi snickered at Nick. "That's what you get for raising your head above the foxhole."

"And Heidi, thanks for raising your head too," Eric cried out. "I want you to work with Nick on this campaign. Get a few more people to help you with it. I want your three best ideas on my desk by Tuesday night so that we can have a solid proposal for the client by Wednesday. Then, if they approve, we will pull the whole thing together in time for the meetings on Friday."

Heidi groaned. She turned and looked inquiringly at Gretchen, who looked her square in the eyes and shook her head no. Eric caught the interplay and asked aloud, "Why don't you want to get in on this, Gretchen?"

She glared at Heidi for a moment for drawing unwanted attention to her, but then spoke loudly enough for the whole group to hear. "Stop and think about the political climate. You have got homeless people sleeping on the sidewalks in the city, and millions of people still living in their homes but unable to pay the bills. And in the middle of all that, you have got a client who is almost openly saying it wants to target the elderly so it can rob them of their life savings in their golden years. It's a recipe for disaster for our client. And as Nick said, it could come back and bite us too."

"What would you suggest?" Eric asked.

Gretchen paused as if she did not want to commit herself, but then plunged in anyway. "The elderly want to leave a legacy for their kids and their grandchildren. They look around and see the misery in the world all around them, right outside their front door. They don't give a shit about monster mining and steel lockboxes, if you will excuse my language. They want to make sure their kids grow up to have secure lives, that they have enough money to pay the bills and stay in their homes. They want to build a lasting legacy for their families."

Nick and Heidi formed O-shapes with their lips, silently mouthing Wow.

"You are onto something here. This could be a game changer," Eric said.

Gretchen, caught up in her own momentum, barely paused to let Eric comment.

"If the client is targeting the elderly—which I think is very risky, but let's give it to them—if the client is going after grandmas and grandpas, then we should not show up in bikinis or short skirts. We should look like their kids and grandkids, wholesome and pure. The difference is, we know something their kids don't about how to create that legacy. How do they set aside enough money to keep the next generations comfortable?"

Heidi laughed and said in a loud mock whisper, "I think that is called raising your head above the foxhole."

Later, as the ambassadors left the room to go back to their desks, Eric called Gretchen over to the corner away from the door. He waited until the others had left the room before he spoke in a low voice.

"Good idea there about how to approach this trading company," he said. Eric glanced over her shoulder toward the door before continuing. "How did things go with Mark Fischer? Does it look like a project you might take on? Is it something you want to bring the full agency in on, or will it be a solo act?"

Gretchen also kept her voice low in case anyone was lingering near the doorway. "I am not sure. He has got some pie-in-the-sky charity idea in mind. I don't know if it is a single event like a fundraiser, or if it is going to turn into several events. I have another meeting scheduled tonight after work, and I will find out more at that time."

Eric eyes lit up. "After work? He asked you out to dinner?"

"Slow down, cowboy," she laughed. "This is a business meeting. We had our initial meet-and-greet at a day-rental office in the city, but that's not his permanent location. So, we are having a follow-up at a restaurant near here where we can discuss it in more detail."

Mark looked interested. "You called it a pie-in-the-sky. Do you think anything will materialize?"

"Like I said, I don't know. He seems serious, and he has got the money. But I would like to see any background research you have on the man, if you are willing to share."

The two of them walked past the ambassadors' workstations to Eric's office in the corner. Closing the door behind herself, Gretchen took a seat and crossed her legs. Eric opened the file drawer on his desk and thumbed through the file tabs. "I suppose I could have forwarded an electronic file to you," he said, "but I prefer not to have it floating around in the ether world of the Internet. Not that I don't trust you, but we have to worry about hackers stealing information on emails."

He opened a file and scanned a few pages. "Mark Fischer, aged 34. Net worth estimated at one point seven billion dollars, as of the close of last year. Single, never married, sexual preference unknown. Parents both died when he was sixteen, doesn't have any siblings. Not known to have involvement in any fraternal, civic, or business organizations other than nominal memberships in several of the usual suspects. No known romantic relationships."

Eric closed the file and passed it over to Gretchen. "It looks like he keeps everything very close to the vest, very private. You will find the basic biography in there, but I think you already know all that stuff. We don't have much on him."

Gretchen took the proffered file folder but did not bother to open it. "No family, no romantic partners, no organizational affiliations. You are telling me we really know nothing about this guy."

"That's about it." Eric put a note of caution in his tone. "Keep in mind that he runs a racetrack. If he doesn't actively participate in organized crime, he probably has a lot of contact with it. He will keep personal information secret so that the bad guys can't find a pressure point to use against him. And watch out yourself, too. If he is running a charitable event, it may be a vehicle for laundering money that he has gotten through illicit means. Do not let yourself get implicated in anything that is going to put you behind bars."

She looked thoughtful. "Did this angle come up when we worked that reception for him recently?"

"Not at all. I just wanted to put it on your radar. He could be trouble."

8

❧

CHAPTER 8

Mark had chosen a restaurant in Half Moon Bay, relatively close to Gretchen's home, so that she would not have to drive far after the meeting was over. The restaurant sat on a cliff overlooking the Pacific Ocean. Well known for its seafood, the fine dining establishment drew a large crowd on weekends for both lunch and dinner. This being a weeknight during the non-tourist season, Mark did not have difficulty getting a reservation. The view outside the window immediately drew their gazes. But Mark quickly returned his focus to Gretchen's eyes.

"Thank you for agreeing to meet me again so soon. I hope this is convenient for you."

"Yes, of course it is. I suspect you know from your research that I live just a few miles from this place. But your home is more than an hour's drive away, isn't it?"

He waved the remark away. "Home isn't important. I will stay at a hotel nearby for the night, and then head down the coast to Santa Cruz for another meeting tomorrow."

The waiter brought a bottle of Zinfandel and poured a sample in Mark's glass. Sniffing the bouquet and taking a sip, Mark nodded his approval and the waiter poured glasses for them both.

"Thank you for being honest yesterday," he said. "I fully understand that trying to solve homelessness sounds like something the homecoming queen would say in her speech at the high school prom."

Gretchen suddenly moved her fingers to her lips to keep from laughing with a mouthful of wine. Catching her breath after swallowing the liquid, she gasped, "I was just thinking that at this very moment, because I think my academic advisor said I should say that solving homelessness and creating world peace was my goal in a speech that I made in high school. But I wasn't the homecoming queen. I delivered the valedictorian's speech." Her eyes narrowed as she looked more intently at him. "Did your background researchers even get the text of my high school graduation speech?"

Now he laughed. "No, that was entirely a coincidence. It just came to mind because I was asked to sit as one of the judges at a beauty pageant a few weeks ago, and no less than three of the contestants said they planned to work to end homelessness."

"Is that what gave you the idea for this project of yours?"

He shook his head faintly. "No, I have been giving this a lot of thought for years."

She took a slice of sourdough from the basket on the table and cut it in half on her bread plate. Then she cut one of the halves in half and spread a thin layer of butter on one of the quarter slices. She nibbled a small bit of it before taking another sip of wine.

"Tell me about your plan."

Mark took a slice of bread too but did not cut it. "As I said, the trickle-down theory was supposed to put more people to work. But it just led to more concentration of money and greed at the top. Hell, well-known people and movie stars were even telling the public that greed is good.

"So, I want to put people to work. I want to create a nonprofit organization that can receive tax-deductible donations. We will start out by hiring homeless people in the city to clean up the streets—collecting trash, steam-cleaning the sidewalks and gutters where garbage or other smelly refuse is fouling the atmosphere. We will pay them to work, under supervision, of course. But we will also have social workers on staff to help them get into temporary housing, set up bank accounts, and get started on establishing credit."

The waiter came and took their orders, thus giving Gretchen a few minutes of distraction to let his words settle into her mind. She buttered a second quarter of her slice of sourdough, to absorb the alcohol of the second glass of wine Mark had just poured for her. She had arrived at the restaurant with an empty stomach and wanted to keep her wits sharp.

"That will probably make you popular with the local merchants. Even though the city government tries to keep the streets clean, they always come up short."

Mark's face brightened. "Who knows? Some of the merchants may even donate to the organization if it makes their neighborhood more attractive to customers. But that's not my primary concern. I want the homeless to experience the pride that comes with working, getting paid for their work and receiving decent benefits, and trying to support themselves. That pride will help them climb even higher after they get back on their feet."

He took another sip of wine. "But the cleanup of the streets is just one aspect. Like I said, we will hire a staff of social workers to help them get set up with the social institutions that the rest of us take for granted. But they will also be doing assessments of the homeless workers' skills. Those homeless people who have the aptitude for teaching can help lead after-school study programs for kids. The people who are good with their hands can be given work on repairs and construction of public facilities that are being neglected by the city's public works department. Those who are good in office work will help run the administration for this organization that we are creating."

The waiter brought their salads. She took a moment to nibble on a bit of lettuce. Gretchen sat up straight. "All this sounds wonderful, and much more promising than I thought when you first told me yesterday. But tell me," she said, "you keep saying we. We are going to do this, and we are going to do that. What part do you want me to play in all of this?"

Mark lifted his napkin to wipe away a bit of blue cheese dressing from the corner of his mouth. He started to speak but caught himself and changed to a more casual tone. "I suppose that, in your line of work, somebody is bound to have told you that you have a lovely face."

Gretchen smiled. "It has come up in conversation a few times. Is that why you asked me out? Because I have a pretty face?"

"No," he said, pausing for a moment. "I was wondering if you could be the face of this organization."

This time, she very nearly did let some of her wine escape her mouth. Holding her napkin against her lips until she could swallow, she recovered and then asked, "The face of the organization. What do you mean, as your spokesperson?"

Mark set down his fork and leaned back in his chair. "Something like that. In the beginning, I think your role would be very much like what you do now. You would serve as a brand ambassador. Of course, since we don't have a brand identity yet, you would be the primary player in establishing our image. Then, if you feel comfortable with it, you would take on more. Instead of just the spokesperson, you could maybe come to be seen as the organization itself."

Gretchen raised an objection. "But why don't you want to be seen as the face of the organization?" she asked. "It is your idea, it is your money, it is your leverage in the business world that will make this succeed, assuming it does succeed. Why not take credit for the good work you are doing? I bet it would create some goodwill for your other businesses, especially the racetrack."

Mark said nothing as a busboy cleared away their salad dishes. He gazed out the window, where the sinking sun was casting a golden glow over the beach. At the height of summer, that beach might still have a large number of people on it soaking up the last of a fun-filled day. But now, just after the annual Indian Summer heat wave of early October had come and gone, the stretch of sand beneath them was nearly empty.

"My face and name would not necessarily add anything good to this venture," he said. "Sure, some people might try to curry favor with me by supporting the effort. But others would deliberately try to sabotage it. So yes, I would be actively involved behind the scenes to line up support from the people who would give it. But I would also work behind the scenes to provide protection against those who would try to undermine us.

"And besides," he added with a grin, "you are much prettier than me. People will donate money when you ask for it. Not so much as when I do."

Gretchen smiled but did not give the customary response. If Mark was fishing for a compliment about his looks, she would not bother giving it because his good looks were already obvious, and she was sure he received compliments from many fawning sycophants. No need for her to join their ranks in a clear example of sucking up to a potential client.

"How would this work?" she asked. "Would you want me to just make a few appearances, pose for pictures and maybe say a few words?"

"I think it would be more than that," he said. "We would need to give you a title as a senior executive. I would need you to be available to make appearances occasionally for more than just a few weeks. Perhaps several months or more."

The waiter brought their entrees. Gretchen's catfish was covered with a light sauce of oil, ginger, and scallions. The vegetables were well cooked but still crisp in their freshness.

"What about my job with the agency? I have put in a number of years with Eric and my colleagues, you know. I would hate to give that up."

Mark used a fork and knife to cut the tail off of a large prawn, and then cut the prawn in half. He raised a bite halfway to his mouth but stopped to glance up into Gretchen's face. "I am not trying to take you away from your world. With careful scheduling, you could probably treat the nonprofit as a side gig while you continued your full-time work with the agency."

"Speaking of the agency," she interrupted, "suppose I need more brand ambassadors to promote the nonprofit's mission. Would I be free to hire them?"

"You would have a budget. Of course, I would expect you to check with me before you enter any binding contracts. But if you need to hire Eric's agency to do some of the work, that would be possible."

Mark set down his fork and leaned forward. "But I want you to know this. If you do hire your agency, it would be you calling the shots, not your boss, Eric. It is not that I don't trust his judgment. But if you are the public face of my nonprofit and its mission, I don't want you thinking that you have to take orders from him. And I would not want you worried about whether you report to him or me on this project. I sign the checks. Is that understood?"

Gretchen looked out the window into the dusk, her eyes unfocused. "I see potential problems. But I agree. That is how it would have to be."

The rest of the dinner passed with casual, non-business conversation. Mark ordered coffee with dessert. He asked for a slice of apple pie. Gretchen ordered only a slice of fresh honeydew melon, with no sweetener or sauce. Both drank their coffee black but did not ask for refills because of the late hour.

"Will you have any problem getting home?" he asked.

"No, I think the coffee and food counteracted the wine, so I am good to drive," she replied. She realized that, though he had rented a hotel room near the restaurant, he apparently was not going to make any attempt to invite her to his room or accompany her to her own home. She wasn't sure whether to feel relief or disappointment at his lack of interest.

They stepped out the door into the parking lot, lit now by overhead streetlights. He accompanied her to his car and, after she had unlocked and opened her door, put out his right hand to shake hers. Then he turned and walked to his own car.

As she pulled out onto the coast highway, Gretchen wondered if she would have felt offended if he had offered a hug instead of the handshake.

9

❧

CHAPTER 9

'Lean forward a bit more to give the camera a view," the photographer said. Gretchen, watching from behind and to the side, understood perfectly what the man was after. He wanted a better picture of Candy's boobs. The bikini top already revealed ample swelling of her breasts above the cut of the material, which was thin enough to clearly show the outlines of her nipples. But the client ran a chain or sports shoe stores, and he had made it plain what he wanted in his promotional shots. Tits and ass. Ass and tits. And if there was enough space to add another picture, more tits.

Candy apparently understood what was going on, because in addition to leaning downward more, she also pulled her arms inward a bit to lift her breasts even higher and accentuate the cleavage. A close look might have revealed to the practiced eye that Candy had applied some makeup to outline her breasts, a hint of shadow to make the valleys look deeper and a bit of highlight to make the mounds look higher. She looked into the camera with her blue eyes and a smile of teeth so white that they could send warning signals in the dark. The photographer clicked off a dozen shots from different angles, glanced at the digital images to make sure they were what he wanted, and then stood up straight. "Okay, I think we have got it. That is it for today."

The rest of the ambassadors put on their robes and started filing out to the dressing room. They had mostly posed for group shots in shorts and halter tops, or bikinis. The client himself had singled out Candy for the closeups. Candy's round firm breasts appeared to defy gravity. Her narrow waist hugged taut abdomen muscles. The cheeks of her rear formed what is popularly called a bubble butt. And her hips were wide enough to accommodate a bronco riding cowboy, as Gretchen was sure they had, many times.

This particular client vetoed any speaking parts for the ambassadors. He had scripted his own voiceover:

"Dudes! Come on down. We have got everything you want, seven days a week." That was it. No words about the superiority of his products, no words about the intelligence or charm of the customers who identified with his brand, no words about his own vision for the world. Just tits and ass. And "dudes."

Gretchen caught Eric's eye while the others were leaving. "I hope you had this guy pay in advance," she said dryly.

"He took the cheapest package we offer that includes this many models," Eric replied. "His results will probably reflect the depth of his planning and business acumen. But speaking of people who know something about business, how are things going with Mark Fischer? Are you going to get some work out of it?"

She raised her eyebrows. "It sounds like it. And there might be some work in it for the agency later too. But first I think I need to sketch out a brand identity and a campaign plan."

"Let me know if you want some help on that. I am here for you."

"Thanks, Eric." She paused for a moment as if considering his offer. "I think I will probably try it on my own at first. When he rejects my proposal, then I will come to you for the expert's suggestion."

Eric looked like he was going to turn and leave, but Gretchen put her hand on his arm. "What more can you tell me about Mark Fischer? He seems an odd one."

Eric shrugged. "All I have got is gossip. Several women in a group I was having drinks with once said they had each made a romantic play for him, but he didn't respond. It is unusual for them to admit that a man had resisted their charms, so they started speculating that he must be gay. But then a few men in the group said they had made a play too but got the same results as the women. So, they started speculating that he must be either asexual or married, or both."

Gretchen laughed out loud. "How typical. They all think, 'If he doesn't make a pass at *me*, then he must have a different sexual preference.' But there's another possibility that they weren't willing to admit out loud. It could be that their own charms are not all as hot as they like to think. Maybe he was not attracted because they just are not attractive?"

"Could be," he agreed, "but I will not be the one to tell them so. I value their company. But while we are on the topic, has he made a play for you? Or vice versa?"

Gretchen held up her hands in a gesture of innocence. "Not a single move, not a single hint, not even a double entendre. I assumed he must be married, but he had a hotel near the restaurant and planned to drive to Santa Cruz the next day. It did not sound like there was anyone waiting for his call at home."

"He had a hotel near the restaurant? It certainly sounds like he was prepared for contingencies with you."

"Oh please, give me credit," she said. "I know what to watch for, better than anyone at the agency. And there was absolutely none of that attitude present."

"Hmm," Mark rubbed his chin. "And how did you feel about that?"

"Maybe I *am* losing my edge. It must be my old age. After all, I am going to be 26 next May." She tried to give a laugh, but it did not sound convincing.

10

∽

CHAPTER 10

She parked on the third basement level in the underground garage at Union Square and rode the elevator up to the ground level. The high-rise hotel where Mark asked to meet her was just across the street, but she decided to pause for a moment to take in the sights. The pandemic had altered the landscape here. Some of the major department stores still had a presence, but several had vacated their locations for less expensive locales outside San Francisco. The walkways still teemed with people strolling through the square, or some, like herself, just standing and looking. Traffic continued as always on the streets on all four borders, with the clang of a bell on a passing cable car on Powell Street.

In the hotel restaurant, Gretchen found Mark sitting at a small table near a window looking out at the city. She joined him and apologized for being late. He waved it away, saying he enjoyed sitting in this spot.

"Union Square looked alive today," she commented, to open the conversation on a light note.

"Yes. A few of the people sitting on the benches had all their belongings in bags next to them, but not so many today. And at least they were sitting on the benches instead of lying on them." Mark snapped out of his mood. "I am sorry, how are you today? I didn't mean to start off sounding so gloomy."

"I feel fine," she said. "And do not worry about it. This is what is on your mind a lot, and this is why we are here today to talk. Are you staying in this hotel tonight?"

"Yes," he said. "I will have some other business meetings, and a reception I am supposed to attend tonight for some politician who would like to separate me from some of my money. I get this a lot, but I have to play the game."

A waitress brought them coffee and lunch menus. "So have you thought about my proposal?" he asked.

"Yes, I have." Gretchen took a sip of coffee. "The first issue is branding. What do we want the public to think when it thinks about this venture? Homelessness? Employment? The city that knows how to get things done? Or Mark Fischer, the Good Guy?"

Mark almost spit out his coffee. "Certainly not that last one. I liked all the others, though."

"No, just choose one. The others will be secondary, but there has to be one overriding image that becomes your brand. This is important. Don't confuse people."

Mark looked uncertain. "What is your recommendation?"

"Clean streets."

"What is your reasoning?"

"If we say we are ending homelessness, nobody will take us seriously. That goal might sound very noble and idealistic, but it is totally impractical. If we make the primary focus employment, then people get bogged down in details—what kind of jobs, how much pay, workers' compensation insurance, payroll reporting, benefits, time and a half for overtime, etcetera. And you said you would form a union of some sort for these people. Well, the unions we already have in this town are going to want to have a hand in that."

Gretchen paused to let her words sink in. "But cleaner streets? Everybody wants that. The people who live here want cleaner streets. The people who commute into the city to work want cleaner streets. Business owners want cleaner streets because it will attract more customers. The tourist bureau wants cleaner streets because it will draw more visitors to the city."

She tapped the table with the tip of her forefinger for emphasis. "And if the cleaner streets program results in giving employment to poor people, so much the better. And if employment of poor people leads to less homelessness, sing hallelujah from the rooftops. And if all this means some people start to think this Mark Fischer guy is okay after all, then that's a nice side benefit too."

"No," he said, "I think we want them to think of Gretchen Vandella, not me. Gretchen Vandella, the beautiful woman with a beautiful heart and a sharp business mind who can make all this happen. What do you think? Are you in?"

Gretchen held the palm of her hand forward as if to say, slow down. "More than me, I think we want them to think of their own collective brilliance. Remember the expression, the City that knows how? Many decades ago, San Franciscans said that with pride. But as for whether I am in, we still don't know what 'in' means. What do you want me to do? How long will it last? Will it leave me enough time to continue my job with the agency?"

Mark nodded as if to acknowledge that he had forgotten to fill in some details. He reached into the inner pocket of his jacket and pulled out a small notebook. "Let me write down a few suggestions, and you can tell me what you think." He scribbled for a moment and tore the small sheet off the rings and placed it on the table between them.

Gretchen turned it over. There was just one word on the page:

President.

She raised her eyebrows and tilted her head. But she kept her silence.

He scribbled on another sheet and tore it off:

Ten thousand dollars per week.

Now she rocked backward and forward in her seat. But still said nothing.

He wrote a bit longer this time before tearing off the sheet:

A minimum of five hours a week. Other than that, as much or as little time as you feel is necessary. You could keep your agency job if you like.

Gretchen folded her arms across her chest and raised one hand to press her fingers against her lips as she stared at the sheet of paper. Then she looked up into Mark's eyes.

He scribbled again, this time on both sides of the paper, and placed the sheet in front of her on the table:

Operating budget of one hundred thousand dollars a month, to start. May increase after fundraising. You select office space, hire support staff, contract with outside help as needed.

Now Gretchen finally broke her silence. "When do I start?"

"I dunno. Are you busy tonight? It occurred to me just a moment ago that you might like to meet this politician."

11

CHAPTER 11

Mark spoke as if he were the host rather than a guest. "Senator, it is good to see you. Let me introduce Ms. Gretchen Vandella. She is the founding president of a new organization called The City That Knows How."

The man, who appeared about 70 years of age but had piercing eyes that looked they never missed a detail, reached out to take her hand. "The City That Knows How? We could certainly stand to bring that back," he said. "Milton Grady, at your service. I represent the northern part of the Peninsula in the state legislature."

"I am very much aware of you and the extensive amount of work you do for the district, Senator. I am one of your constituents, from Pacifica."

The politician beamed. "So glad to meet you, Gretchen. So, tell me about The City That Knows How."

Her glass contained real wine rather than colored water, so Gretchen took only a small sip before speaking. "We are going to bring clean streets back to the city, Senator. We are going to employ the homeless and underhoused to pick up trash, scrub the sidewalks, and I hope they even have time to polish the Walk buttons on the traffic signal poles."

The man chuckled but leaned forward to speak in a lower voice. "Employ the homeless, you say?"

"Yes, give them regular jobs with good pay. We will help them get established with bank accounts, and when they have saved enough money, get them into their own places to live. But all of that will take much more time. The first issue is to get the streets clean."

The senator slipped a business card to Gretchen. "Give my office a call next week. I would like to learn more about your organization." He smiled and nodded at her and Mark before moving away to speak to another guest.

Mark discreetly smiled. "I think you made an impression. He invited you to call and make an appointment. He does not do that with everyone that he meets."

Gretchen nodded subtly. "That alone may call for a celebration later." She looked directly into his eyes as she said this. But if he thought she might be dropping a hint for some personal time for a "celebration" to-gether, he did not seem to give any indication in his expression or body English. Though she had joked with Eric that she might be losing her edge, Gretchen began to wonder if it might be true. She recalled Eric mentioning that a number of women and men had also failed to elicit any interest from Mark, but she refused to put herself in the same class as them. She was a professional. Eliciting interest from a man was no casual matter to her. It defined her very being.

Mark's attention was diverted across the room. "Oh, do you see that woman near the buffet? She serves on the public works commission, which currently has responsibility for cleaning all public areas. Let me introduce you, because her vote could be crucial to letting us proceed with our plans. After all, we would be doing some of the work her department's employees are currently responsible for." Without waiting for her reply, he started moving across the room. Like a student being led by the teacher on a field trip, Gretchen dutifully followed along.

Later, after politely sampling several cheese cubes, celery sticks, and even stabbing a marinated shrimp with a toothpick, Gretchen found she had finished her glass of wine and needed to accept the offer of a new glass from a waitress passing by with a tray. She barely wet her lips with a few drops.

A matron was chattering away with her about the difficulty to find trustworthy and reliable housekeeping and gardening staff. Gretchen half listened but found her eye wandering. This elderly woman could be important in generating financial support from the wealthy class, so Gretchen needed to keep this conversation going as long as necessary. But she saw members of city government in the room who might have a more immediate impact on her mission, so she kept an ear open for an opportunity to extricate herself. At some point, the matron would have to pause in her monologue, if for no other reason, to at least inhale some air.

"My dear, could I steal you away over here for a few minutes?" The sound of Mark's voice from behind her nearly caused a fluttering of her heart. Gretchen wondered to herself, is it just because it means I can get away from this woman and her housekeeping staff worries? Or was it because it meant I would get back to spending time with him?

Gretchen apologized to the elderly woman and said she would try to return if she was able. She walked with Mark back toward a less crowded corner of the room, where they stopped to confer.

"What do you think?" she asked. "I have chatted with a number of people who can open some doors for us. Do you want me to continue?"

Mark grinned. "That's just it. I have overheard a few conversations that took place after you have left this or that person to go somewhere else. Others were coming up to them afterward and asking who you were. And I saw a few of them take out their phones to take pictures of you. So maybe you have already created some buzz. But you are the expert. Do you want to stay, or would you prefer to get out of here?"

She scanned the faces across the room looking to see if any major dignitaries remained. "If that's the case, then we could get out early. If we stay too long, we look desperate. But if there is already a bit of buzz going around, then we can leave and create an air of mystery."

He nodded. "Thank God. Let's get out of here."

When they stepped out front, Mark tipped the valet to go pick up his car. "You are still parked back at Union Square, aren't you? That's where I am going, back to the hotel. Do you have time to stop in for either a drink or a coffee to debrief?"

"Absolutely. I think it would be a good idea to compare notes so we can plan where to go and what to do next." She sank into the leather bucket seat and fastened her seatbelt for the slow ride up and down the intervening hills. And Mark seemed happy to be taking it slow, gliding through Pacific Heights, up Russian Hill, over Nob Hill and then down to Union Square. He took a ticket from the hotel's valet as he and Gretchen got out of the car and strolled through the entrance and across the lobby to the entrance to the bar. They took a seat at a table in the corner.

Mark ordered an Irish Coffee, so Gretchen asked for the same. They discussed conversations they had with various individuals at the reception earlier and jotted down a list of contacts that she would follow up with later. First and foremost, would be the call to the state senator's office to set up a meeting. That meeting could lead to developments that would open doors to many other influential figures.

"I think this went extremely well," Mark commented as he sipped some of his drink, the whipped cream sticking to his upper lip like a white moustache. "Considering you have been president for less than a day, you have certainly proven your worth. Oh, that reminds me," he said, reaching into his jacket pocket. He pulled out a checkbook and a pen. "I know it is customary to pay you at the end of a week's work. But you earned your keep tonight, and more."

Gretchen only glanced at the check to confirm the amount, $10,000, before slipping it into her purse. She continued writing names on her list of people to call or see in the coming weeks. The Irish coffee satisfied her craving for a touch more alcohol but at the same time woke her up from the lethargy that often comes at the end of the night.

Finally, Mark leaned on one elbow casually. "Well, can I walk you to your car?"

Gretchen hoped she had not physically flinched in response. Calling it a night so soon? It had seemed that he might—well, maybe it was best not to go where her imagination had been drifting. Too soon, and this was business, not personal.

Not wishing to let her walk alone in the night, even if her garage was just across the street, Mark accompanied her to the elevator in the plaza and rode down with her to the third floor. They walked together to her car, and she pressed the button on her key fob to unlock the door. She turned around to face him.

"A wonderful beginning," Mark said, reaching out to shake her hand. She clasped his hand lightly. He made no move to get closer, so she released his hand, turned and sat in the driver's seat. She closed the door and opened her window. "Should I call you tomorrow?"

He shook his head. "Go ahead to your job at the agency. We will touch bases either in the evening or the next day." With that, he waved and turned to walk back to the elevator.

She sat in her car watching his back as he walked a steady pace back the way they had come together moments earlier. No spring in his step, no skipping or any sign of any emotion good or bad. Nothing.

With a sigh, she turned on the ignition and backed out of her parking space. As she shifted into drive, she saw him enter the elevator, and the door closed behind him. She drove up the ramp toward the exit.

* * *

As she entered the front door of her condo, Gretchen snapped on the light and looked around. Everything in its place, as always. She set her purse down and sat on the couch, turning on her iPad. She navigated to the text field on her social media account, and typed a new message:

"Hey, baby, I was thinking of you tonight. How are you?"

Then she attached a five-second closeup selfie video clip of herself in a very low-cut bikini, turning from side to side to emphasize every bit of her cleavage. Reviewing the video clip, she approved of the pouting lips, the eyes staring seductively into the camera. And her boobs. They were perfect.

Gretchen clicked the "To" field on the message and addressed the text and video to a distribution list of lonely men who followed her on this application. She clicked the Send button.

Gretchen got up and took off her clothes. Though she would be sleeping alone tonight, as she had done almost every night for all of the past eight years, she selected a very sexy looking lace nightie. Turning sideways to see her profile in the mirror, she was tempted to take a picture with her camera. Just then, the screen of the iPad lit up as a response to her text came in. She picked up the pad and looked. Already, more than a dozen had excitedly responded. "Beautiful!" said one. "I will dream of you tonight, Sweetcakes," said another. "I am yours to command, my Lady," read the third.

Smiling as more text responses came in, Gretchen made a decision. She stood in front of the full-length mirror in her negligee, held the iPad out to her right, outside the frame of the picture, and clicked off several shots. Selecting the most alluring of the pictures, she attached it to a new text message. "I am going to bed now, but I will be thinking of you." She addressed it to the same distribution list of lonely men and clicked Send.

Gretchen set the iPad on the dresser in her bedroom. She turned off the lights and settled into bed. As she let the day's tensions fade from her psyche, she saw the glow of the iPad screen reflect off the ceiling repeatedly as her legion of lonely men sent responses back saying they would be thinking of her too.

Smiling, she closed her eyes to go to sleep.

12

CHAPTER 12

One of the young women who worked on the photography crew was tightening the screw on a pole after hoisting the spotlight up to a height of about eight feet. "Ladies," she called out, "make sure the gloss on your lower lips does not reflect too much light back at the camera. We want them to look moist, not metallic."

Melanie and Gretchen checked their lips in the mirror. They each wore the same shade because it reflected well off of their light olive complexions. Gretchen wore an elegant gown with a plunging neckline for the shoot today. Melanie's gown featured a higher neckline, but discreet stitching pulled the fabric tight at the midriff and lifted her breasts prominently. Both women had conditioned their dark hair to shine lustrously.

"How are you doing today, sweetie," Melanie asked. "I have been pretty frazzled lately. To be honest, I can't even remember what business we are promoting with this shoot."

"It is a high-end men's clothing brand," Gretchen replied. "They'll take pictures of you and me separately and together. I think they might even have Mario putting on a white tie outfit for shots with each of us."

"That's nice. I like Mario."

"But you asked how I am today!" Gretchen sighed. "I am starting to wonder if I am losing it. Maybe I am getting old."

Melanie looked at her colleague sideways. "Oh, honey, you are definitely not losing it. You know you are still the number one Ambassador on this crew."

"Yeah, but there's this guy."

"Ooh, there's a guy! Something hot going on in the wonderful life of the star, Gretchen?"

"No, that's just it. Nothing is going on. Absolutely nothing."

Melanie pulled her head back as if in disbelief. "Is he married? Is he gay? Is he having an operation so he can switch sides?"

Gretchen smiled at the gag. "Not that I can tell. He doesn't seem to have any of those issue. And even with people dealing with issues like that, I can usually get some sort of response. But with this one? Nothing. Not a blink."

The photographer, also a woman, directed the two of them to a spot in the studio with a white backdrop. After positioning themselves, Gretchen and Melanie each turned left and right while keeping their faces pointed toward the camera. Then they each did the same for solo poses. The photographer then climbed a stepladder so she could shoot the same set of poses from a vantage point three feet above the models as they looked upward at the lens.

"So how did this man come into your field of vision?" Melanie asked after the photographer climbed down. They would wait for Mario to join them, for a new set of shots. It being a session for a men's fashion line, they knew that they should expect pictures of him with both of them on either of his arms, and separately. And in addition to the usual poses with the women looking directly into the camera, they would do a set of pictures gazing at him as if they were adoring him or undressing him with their eyes. Fortunately, Mario fit the bill nicely anyway, so such poses would not force a stretch of the imagination.

"It was business," Gretchen said. "And we have maintained a strictly businesslike acquaintance. But you know how it goes," she added, turning to look at Melanie. "No matter how businesslike, there's always something hanging over you in the background. There's always an urge to touch, and maybe more than touch. You know what they are thinking.

They always want to carve a notch in their bed post. But this one hasn't made a move."

Melanie stopped and faced Gretchen directly. "Do you like him?"

Gretchen opened her mouth slightly as if to reply but exhaled loudly instead. Glancing downward to her left as if she might find the answer on her shoulder, she muttered, "I don't know. I really don't know."

13

❧

CHAPTER 13

Not that she objected to the agency getting more business, but Gretchen wondered why today's client had bothered hiring them at a cost that would certainly run much higher than a standard modeling agency. The client manufactured surfboards, so of course the entire crew dressed in swimsuits for an outdoor shoot at the beach. Lots of flesh and smiling faces. Lots of sand, lots of waves. There was no "management" of a brand image or identity here, at least to her thinking. Surfers rode waves, they didn't discuss philosophy or try to save the world. The client could have just hired models.

But hey—he was paying for brand ambassadors, so that's what he would get. They all tried to look the parts they played most often on their other assignments—Gretchen and Melanie the dark beauties, Heidi the vulnerable maiden in distress, Candy the blonde bombshell, and so forth. The men were here today too—some of them looking like body-builders, some like construction workers, one or two like executives who did not get out in the sun very often. Two of the bodybuilders stood next to a couple of the client's surfboards held standing on end with the logo visible.

They finished the shoot rather quickly, and the ambassadors put on shirts or robes to ward off the sun. Even though they all wore sunscreen —Candy too, after a stern lecture from Eric following her burn in San

60

Diego—none wanted to dare the fates to deliver any damage from exposure to the elements. And not just the sun—despite the protective perimeter they had set up to cordon off the area, plenty of regular beachgoers were throwing frisbees and footballs, objects that could leave a bruise or perhaps even break the skin if they hit one of the ambassadors. Better to pack up and go back to the office quicky than to risk a mishap that could ruin their appeal for the camera, if even only for a day or two.

As the ambassadors lined up to board the bus back to the office, Candy glanced over her shoulder to see who was behind her. "Ah, it is Gretchen. What's this I hear that your animal magnetism has failed to attract an animal?"

Gretchen gave her head a shake as if she had not heard correctly. "What did you say?"

"I heard there was some hot guy, and you couldn't even get a rise out of him."

Gretchen tried to keep the shock out of her voice. "Who said that?"

Candy laughed. "Everyone's saying it, babe. I guess I shouldn't have said anything. I thought you already knew that you were the topic of the day."

By now a few of the other people in line had overheard and threw surreptitious glances over their shoulders at Candy and Gretchen but kept quiet.

Before saying anything, Gretchen forced herself to stay calm. "A lot of fuss over nothing. It was just somebody I chatted with once or twice."

"Ohhhhh–kaaaay, if you say so," Candy intoned a bit too loudly for Gretchen's taste. Then, in a softer voice, she added, "But that's not what I heard."

Gretchen took a seat at the front of the bus, scooting over toward the window to make room for anyone who wanted to sit next to her. The other ambassadors and staff filed up the center aisle toward the back of the bus.

As the last of her coworkers filled in the seats to the rear and the spot on the bench next to her remained empty, Gretchen heard Candy, a few rows behind her, say in a none-too-quiet whisper, "So, I hear the Ice Queen got frozen out herself."

Another voiced hissed to hush her. "Don't call her that. You don't know what happened to her."

"Musta been pretty bad. She has got absolutely no emotion," Candy replied.

Gretchen did not let a muscle on her face move, nor did she flinch or show any physical reaction. She had long since learned not to give any detractors the satisfaction of a pained response.

* * *

The day had finally arrived to attend her first high school dance, and sixteen-year-old Gretchen felt both excitement and nervousness. She had practiced the latest dance steps alone in front of the full-length mirror in her bedroom while playing hip-hop songs on her CD player. She had selected an alluring outfit that did not actually show any of her ample cleavage but nonetheless emphasized the shape and curves of her breasts. And now, in the school gym with recorded music blaring over the tinny-sounding public address system, she stood on one side of the room where the girls congregated together, while the boys mostly stood near the wall on the opposite side of the basketball court. Finally losing patience for any of the boys to summon the courage to ask them to dance, a few of the girls started dancing together in the center of the gym at what would be mid-court during a basketball game.

Seeing the girls dancing, three boys ventured across the room to timidly ask girls if they would like to try a song with them. With the addition of a few mixed couples. the dance floor slowly began to fill up.

Derek, a cute boy but something of a self-absorbed jock, approached Gretchen and invited her out onto the floor. They swayed back and forth, she demonstrating what she had taught herself at home, he demonstrating that he really did not have a clue about the relationship between the rhythm of the music and the rhythm of his bodily movements. But she enjoyed it anyway, and after the song was over, the two of them spoke together away from the other dancers. When the music started up again, they could not hear each other's voices, so Derek motioned toward the door.

Outside, he suggested they stroll toward the classrooms. Happy to get fresh air after the stuffiness in a gym full of people, Gretchen followed along. They turned past a row of student lockers toward the first room, where Gretchen's English class met during second period each morning. Derek turned the knob on the door, and to Gretchen's surprise, it opened. She peered inside, and then felt Derek's hand against her back pushing her into the room.

The lights went on, and Gretchen found herself surrounded by Derek and three other boys. They started giggling to themselves. One behind her squeezed the left cheek of Gretchen's butt. She squealed and spun around at the boy, yelling, "Keep your hands off me, you pervert!"

But even as she yelled at him, one of the other boys reached around her side and clutched her left breast. Another boy reached from the other side and squeezed her right breast. The fourth boy, apparently Derek, lifted her skirt from behind and reached underneath to press his fingers against the front of her panties.

Gretchen screamed.

"Aw, come on, babe, just relax and enjoy it," one of the boys said. Another one laughed and grunted his agreement.

Whack!

The sharp crack of wood against flesh made a loud thud, and the boy who received the blow cried out in pain. A thud hit another one of the boys in the shoulder, and he yelled, "What the fuck?" All the boys turned and found themselves looking at Miss Granger, the girls' gym coach. She held a baseball bat like a homerun slugger and looked prepared to do them some damage. The boys fled from the room.

"Are you okay, honey? Do you need me to call an ambulance?" Miss Granger asked.

"No, I am just shaken up. Other than putting their hands on me, they didn't get any farther. I am glad you showed up."

"I got suspicious when I saw that boy take you out of the dance and lead you to a secluded area. I should call the police. That was a sexual assault, and you should press charges so they never do it again."

Gretchen pleaded with the teacher. "No, please don't call the police. Nothing will happen to those boys, and I'm afraid to get involved in a police matter."

The teacher shook her head. "I understand your concern, but I have to tell you that these boys had this planned. They will try to do it again to another girl. Do you know their names?"

"Just the one," Gretchen said. "His name is Derek, but I don't know his last name. I don't think I have ever met or heard the names of the other three."

"Well, even if you won't report it, I will report it to the vice principal's office and the campus security. These boys will be dealt with. In the meantime, honey, take good care of yourself and learn to think defensively. You are very attractive, which means assholes like those boys will try to take advantage of you every chance they get."

Gretchen nodded. "Yes, Ma'am. I will be careful from now on."

* * *

Eric boarded the bus after all the ambassadors and, seeing the back seats all taken, sat next to Gretchen on the front padded bench. The bus driver started the engine and pulled away from the curb.

"We haven't talked for several days. How have you been?" Eric asked.

"Good," she replied quickly. "Keeping an eye on the road ahead, keeping track of whom I can trust, and whom I should not."

"Smart lady," he quipped. "Maybe when we get back to the office, you and I can find time to chat. I would like to hear more about what you have been up to."

She nodded. "I would like that. There have been some developments."

"Anything that will affect our crew here?"

"I am not sure yet." She stared at the back of the bus driver's head. "Like I said, I am keeping track of some things. And keeping track of some people. I will let you know what develops."

The ride back to the office only took twenty minutes because the heavy traffic would not start for several hours yet. The office occupied a large space in a former neighborhood movie theater. Decades earlier, many San Francisco neighborhoods boasted their own local, independent movie houses, but those days had long since passed as multi-screen complexes took over the business. Even the large complexes had suffered during the pandemic as an increasing share of the public grew accustomed to cable TV or live-streaming video channels at home. The agency shared the old theater building with a small accounting office that faced the street on the ground level; the agency had its photography studio in the former theater space and built offices at the mezzanine level and in the old projection room. When they took over the building, Eric had walled off the office from the studio and had contractors put in windows facing outside to take the gloom out of the office area.

After changing into her street clothes and putting her bikini in a tote bag to take home for laundering, Gretchen glanced quickly at her desk. Nothing pressing in the In tray, no alerts on the computer, no text messages. She stood up from her desk and walked over to Eric's office. He had his phone pressed to his ear but motioned for her to sit.

Eric said a few words to finish his call, and then hung up. "Do you want to close the door?"

She did so and resumed her seat. "I gotta say, I don't think we did a lot to create a brand identity for Armstrong Surfboards today."

"Yeah, he could have just hired a few models. But I wasn't going to turn him away." Eric shifted his posture in his desk chair. "I thought I should check in to see how your talks with Mark Fischer are going."

"Oh that. I thought you wanted to discuss a branding project for a motorcycle shop," Gretchen joked. She knew quite well what he wanted to talk about, and he knew she knew.

She sat up straight and put on an officious air. "I will have you know that you are addressing the new president of The City That Knows How. If I ever get a ring, I will allow you to kiss it."

"Come on, I was being serious," Eric said.

"So was I. Mark is creating a nonprofit called The City That Knows

How, and I am the president. I accepted payment, so I guess that makes it official."

Eric held his palms facing up toward the ceiling as if asking a question, so Gretchen filled him in on Mark's vision. Then she told him about the politician's reception, and the contacts she had already made.

"I haven't fully developed the brand yet. I told him we would focus the brand on clean streets, and the other bits would be side benefits that would add to the mission but not distract from it."

"Smart thinking. Focus on one image, and let the secondary images fill in the gaps on the sides as they become available," he said. "So does this mean you are quitting?"

"Oh God, no. He set this up as a side gig for me. There may be some days that I am not available here, but I will be as careful as possible with scheduling to avoid that. In fact, I may end up hiring the agency to do some projects. He is going to give me a budget."

Suddenly, Eric took more interest. Hearing the word budget snapped him to attention. "What do you think we will be doing? Promo shots?"

Gretchen gave a short laugh. "Somehow, I can't picture our ambassadors dressed in bikinis picking up trash off the streets of San Francisco. For one thing, the weather is too cold."

"No, you are right about that."

"But maybe we could have the ambassadors attend social and political events, promoting the brand's bullet points. It never hurts to have pretty faces and solid-looking men advocating your point of view."

The two of them sketched a simple flow chart on a sheet of paper. Having ideas on paper made it easier for Gretchen to formulate a plan. "That looks good," she said, pointing at one section, "but I think this one over here might cheapen the mission and make it look like just a cheesy marketing campaign. I want people coming away from this feeling civic pride, not erotic cravings."

"I see your point,"" Eric laughed. "But don't forget, a horny donor is a generous donor."

"Yes," she agreed, "but sometimes somebody who signs a check while horny stops payment on it after the feeling fades. Or at least feels like he or she was taken for a fool, and never writes another check. Besides, I think Mark is going to be soliciting donations from large donors and organizations that want tax deductions and favorable publicity, not just tits and ass."

After forty-five minutes, they put down their pencils and exhaled. "I am sorry, I didn't mean to take advantage of your generosity here," she said.

"Hey, I owe some free consultation to you. Speaking of which, do you remember that crypto trading company with the data mining artificial intelligence? They absolutely loved your idea about investors building a fortune to leave for their children and grandchildren. They've signed a contract to have our people speak at a dozen seminars specifically targeting investors in senior retirement communities. Do you want to get in on it?"

"No, I don't think I will have time," Gretchen said. "And even if it sounds more palatable to say they're building a legacy for the next generation, I still don't like hustling the elderly for their savings."

"Understood. Then I won't assign you to any of their events."

14

❧

CHAPTER 14

"Hi, my name is Greg Black. Please have a seat. The senator asked me to meet with you to hear about your proposal. As I understand it, you want to apply for state funds for a street cleanup project. Is that correct?"

Gretchen handed Greg one of her newly printed business cards. Gretchen Vandella, President, The City That Knows How. It bore the same address as Eric's agency; she was having an office built in the ground-floor corner that the box office and concession stand used to occupy. She would have a contractor build an entrance separate from that of the accountant's office, and she would have her own washroom installed. Eric had called upon a contractor who owed him a favor, who was getting the work finished as quickly as possible because he had only taken out a permit to install storage facilities in the empty space on the ground floor next door to the accountant. If his workers and equipment remained at the site for more than a few days, the city inspector cruising by might stop to ask what was causing the delay on such a simple job. Gretchen had already ordered office furniture, which would be delivered the following week.

"Hi, Greg, I am Gretchen Vandella. I think someone mischaracterized my organization. We are not applying for tax money. We plan to run a street cleanup program at no charge to the public. The senator asked me for this meeting after he heard about our plans."

68

"I see," he responded, looking down at his handwritten notes, and then glancing at her business card. "This is a nonprofit? Where are you getting your funds?"

Gretchen gave a wide smile. She had anticipated this question. "A number of very generous donors have set up this program. They want to restore the city to its days of glory. It will be good for the city, and good for business. In turn, it will be good for the people who live in the senator's district."

"Yes," he said, "but who is providing the money?"

"You can understand that they wish to remain anonymous for now," Gretchen continued smiling broadly. "For one thing, if it becomes known how much they are donating for this mission, then every nonprofit in the country will swoop down on them begging for money for their own projects. But also, they don't want to become the focus. Rather than appreciating the good work that is being done, people would harp on how rich the donors are and ask why they aren't giving more, and for other problems the city is facing too. We want to focus on this single issue for now, without distractions."

Greg gave her a look that could have been suspicion, but he covered it up with a neutral tone. "I see. Then what can I do for you today?"

Gretchen had also anticipated this question. In fact, she had designed her approach to the meeting around this very question, and she had committed a short wish list to memory.

"We plan to offer jobs to homeless people to clean up the streets, paying double the national minimum wage," she started. Greg leaned forward a bit when she mentioned employing the homeless and the wages she would pay. "Recruiting will require a structured approach. We could just have a bunch of our people approach homeless people they see on the street and make the offer, but the workers will require supervision; paperwork needs to be completed and filed to properly record who is working and getting paid; payroll services to deduct income taxes and so forth. Just the personnel side of this venture alone will require a lot of help, so I was hoping the senator's office could help line me up with some services that could accomplish this. I would ordinarily approach some people I know in city government, but the senator asked me to consult with him first."

Gretchen had come into this meeting hoping to offer something for free. Not only the city cleaning program, but also the opportunity for the politician to offer jobs to allies. He could dispense favors like currency, and the recipients would be in the senator's debt. And political debt really was currency.

If Greg still felt suspicious about the source of funding for Gretchen's nonprofit organization, he no longer seemed worried. "Yes, we know several good candidates for these responsibilities, both in the private sector and in the nonprofit arena. I think we could set you up with something. And of course, when you launch your program, the senator would like to appear with you at a press conference to help publicize it."

"Of course, the senator's help in that regard would be invaluable," Gretchen said. "I am counting on it."

* * *

Later, back in her cubicle at Eric's agency, she made a call to Mark's cell phone. She told him the senator's staff would play ball on helping to set up the infrastructure for personnel services. She would contact the mayor's office on making a deal with the public works department, as well as the health department to provide healthcare coverage for the new workers. Then she would contact staff for each member of the Board of Supervisors, to determine what favors each would like to extract from her in return for supporting the mission. She would also touch bases with the state Assembly members to gain additional support in Sacramento.

Afterward, she looked at her notes and started penciling appointments on her calendar. She said aloud to herself, "When I told Eric I would be careful about scheduling, I lied."

15

The size of the crowd did not intimidate her. Only about a hundred and fifty people stood around the semicircular base of the grand marble staircase in the center of San Francisco's City Hall. She had spoken to larger crowds many times in her role as a brand ambassador for various clients. Though most observers discounted the ambassadors as nothing more than photogenic airheads with long legs and outstanding bustlines, each of them had an impressive resume of academic and public performance achievements. Eric's Aurora Marketing Agency would never have granted them job interviews, let alone permanent positions of employment, if they did not have sterling credentials. Gretchen had a long history of giving speeches before groups both big and small, of both consumers and business leaders.

But she felt nervous, nevertheless. This crowd had not gathered to hear her speak about a client. This crowd had come out today specifically to see and listen to *her*. A new player had appeared on the scene, an organization with the audacious name of The City That Knows How, and the president was a beautiful woman with a brain, or so reliable sources had reported. Just who was this Gretchen Vandella, and what did she have to say that would spark any interest beyond a single day's headline?

A dozen cameras flashed as she stepped up to the dais that had been set up on the first landing of the staircase. Almost every single day of the year, newlywed couples stood on this very landing to have their wedding pictures taken. The grand staircase, the high, sweeping ceiling, the grandeur of the place seemed larger than life. The photos taken of her here this morning would live on for as long as the nonprofit continued.

She had asked that a low table with a banner reading, The City That Knows How, be set up rather than a traditional podium. Gretchen had a cordless mike attached to her business jacket. She did not want to stand behind a podium that would hide her body from the cameras or speak into a bank of microphones that would result in photos giving the appearance that she was about to put one of the mics into her mouth. Her crew had given the TV and radio reporters a direct link into the sound system Gretchen was using, so multiple microphones for each of their recorders would not be necessary. She wanted to use all of her assets today, and her physical appearance stood out as the most obvious.

Gretchen looked out over the crowd and could pick out Aurora's ambassadors scattered evenly among the people. As she had requested, about half came dressed in business smart casual attire while the other half wore street casual, looking more like low-wage workers who had come into City Hall during their lunch breaks. She wanted the press to believe that she was attracting both the working class and the political elite.

"Thank you, Mayor Blum, for those kind words," she said, nodding to the man who had just introduced her to the crowd as one of the brightest young minds he had met in his many years of public service. His introductory remarks, stretching on for more than five minutes, had neatly set up all three major talking points: Clean streets. Work and benefits for the homeless. No taxpayer expense at all. She had asked his staff to keep it simple, and they came through perfectly. "I am so glad to have your support and that of your administration," she added.

Gretchen turned to face the crowd.

"After the Earthquake and Fire of 1906, San Francisco declared to the world that it would rebuild and be reborn. And so it was. And just eleven years later when America entered World War I in 1917, San Francisco proved to the world that it was 'the city that knows how.' San Francisco got things done. It helped preserve the world during and after the Great

War. Though other cities on the West Coast had much larger populations and much larger size, the world learned to look to San Francisco for solutions. It was no coincidence that in 1945 as the Second World War wound down, the United Nations was created at a conference here in San Francisco, just across the plaza on the other side of Polk Street outside the doors behind you."

She paused for a moment to let her words sink in. This took balls, comparing her organization's mission to the birth of the United Nations and the city's history of grit and survival. She glanced toward the back of the crowd and saw Mark Fischer nodding his approval. He stood close to another well-dressed man whom Gretchen vaguely recognized but whose name she could not quite put her finger on. But she could not allow herself to get distracted.

"We have gone through some hard times lately, and it shows. Retail establishments took a severe hit during the pandemic. The decline of so many high technology companies took a chunk out of the city's tax base and hurt the small businesses that depended so much on the tech work-ers. But now the time has come to pull ourselves up by the bootstraps," she said. "This is the city that knows how. The first thing we are going to do is clean up the streets. The public works department does a wonder-ful job trying to keep the streets clean, but it has been overwhelmed by the huge volume of trash that people carelessly drop, and the amount of waste that piles up.

"And as the mayor said, we are going to hire people who are either homeless or underhoused. Many of them live on the streets now, and they are well aware of the problems on the streets and probably have a lot of ideas themselves about what needs to be done. So, we are going to put them to work to help solve it. We will pay them well and they will have the pride that comes with working to support themselves. We will help them get set up in housing that they can pay for themselves."

Gretchen paused again. This next talking point would drive the issue but would also generate the most questions. She had artfully dodged the questions before now. Would her luck continue? She glanced toward

Mark at the back again, but he was leaning toward the other man in what appeared to be a deep discussion.

"Most important to Mayor Blum and the other people here in City Hall, we will do this without using a penny of city taxpayer funds. The City That Knows How has established itself as a nonprofit organization, meaning you can make tax-deductible donations to support our mission. Just go to our website and click the link to donate. A number of very generous donors have already graciously given enough money to seed the program and get it off the ground. I am confident that after they begin to see results, the people of San Francisco will also contribute toward our goal. After all, San Franciscans, we are the city that knows how. And we will again show the world how it is done."

After a brief moment, Gretchen said, "And now, I have a few minutes to answer any questions you may have."

Several hands went up immediately, but Gretchen called on Melanie of Aurora's staff before any reporters had time to shout out questions without waiting to be called on. Gretchen had scripted Melanie's question in advance.

"Ms. Vandella, you said you are going to hire the homeless. How will you recruit them, and how much are you going to pay them?"

Gretchen waved her hand in the air to signal the importance of this question. "Recruitment will be handled by several existing nonprofit agencies that already work with the homeless population here," she replied. "We will be paying the workers double the national minimum wage, so we did not want there to be any chance of fraud or abuse. These agencies already know who is on the street, who can be trusted to do the work if given the opportunity, and who can help bring others along on the path to self-sufficiency."

She quickly called on Nick before reporters could interrupt. Nick had dressed like a regular guy off the street, but his good looks stood out. Gretchen already knew what the question would be.

"Every day I walk past dozens of people sleeping on the sidewalk or laying down on park benches. Are you telling us that all these people are going to be off the streets now?"

"Absolutely not," Gretchen said loudly into her mic. "We cannot solve the whole homeless problem in a day, or even in a year. We can only hope to make a significant dent in it. But with your support, the program will continue to grow, and we will put more and more people to work."

She quickly pointed at Heidi.

"This sounds great," Heidi said. "If my friends and I want to volunteer to help out, what should we do?"

Gretchen smiled broadly. "I am glad you asked. Just go to our website, city that knows how dot org, and click the how to help button. That's city that knows how dot org, with no spaces," she repeated the URL slowly. "That's all the time we have at this moment. Thank you so much for coming out today. We will keep you posted on our progress."

Gretchen reached back to the control set mounted on her belt on the small of her back and turned off the mic. Then she reached out to shake hands with the mayor, who pulled her close to whisper in her ear.

"Well spoken," the mayor said in a low voice. "But do you know that man standing near the back, Mark Fischer?"

"Yes, I do," Gretchen replied quietly. "In fact, he is one of our major donors."

"Well," the mayor continued, "that man he has been talking to all through this presentation is Mikal Popov, the head of the local Russian mob. You'd better be very careful about the sources of your funding, or else I will withdraw the city's support. And if you have gotten me implicated in anything shady here, I will make sure you crash and burn." The mayor kept a bright smile on his face while he whispered, for the benefit of the cameras. Gretchen, too, kept her smile frozen on her face. But her eyes lost their focus as the cameras flashed.

* * *

Sixteen-year-old Gretchen had arrived on campus too late to stop at her locker, so she had all the books and papers she had taken with her the previous night for homework. She sat in her homeroom class half listening to the teacher read the day's school announcements while she scanned through her notes and once again went over the sequence of her homework assignments to be turned in to her subsequent classes today. A girl entered the room and approached the teacher's desk with a slip of paper that Gretchen recognized as an office summons. The teacher took it from the girl, read the slip for a moment, and then called out, "Gretchen Vandella, report to the office. We are going to be finished here in ten minutes, so you should take your books and sweater with you."

Gretchen took the slip of paper from the teacher and carried her books and belongings out the door. She stopped at her locker in the hallway and dropped off the textbooks and homework assignments she would not need to carry with her to the next class. Having a lighter load now, she set off for the school's administrative office.

Two clerks looked up from their computer screens at their desks when Gretchen entered the office. One of them recognized her and pointed to the rear of the room. "Miss Granger, she's here."

The physical education instructor motioned to Gretchen to accompany her. Gretchen stepped through the swinging wooden "gate" into the work area and navigated between the desks toward where the teacher beckoned.

"I told the vice principal a bit of what happened Friday night at the dance, but he needs to hear the full story from you," Miss Granger said. "Don't worry, honey, I will be there with you."

Mr. Beck did not have a large office, but he had two chairs for visitors. Gretchen sat on the chair next to the wall, and Miss Granger took the seat next to her. Gretchen belatedly realized that she was thus boxed in and would only be able to leave when the teacher got up to make room. But fortunately, Miss Granger was on her side, so Gretchen felt at ease.

Gretchen told the story of how Derek had suggested they leave the stuffiness of the gym to get some fresh air, and then lured her to a classroom where three of his buddies were waiting in secret. Derek opened the door and pushed Gretchen into the arms of the other boys, who immediately began putting their hands on her breasts, pinching her hips and buttocks, and then one of the boys pressed his fingers against her vagina. At that point, Miss Granger intervened, and the boys fled the scene.

"Do you know the boys' names?" he asked.

"The boy who took me to the room is named Derek, but I do not know his last name or any of the names of the others," the girl answered.

Mr. Beck reached into a drawer and pulled out the school yearbook from the previous year. "This will not have the pictures of the current freshman class, but you can look over the upper classes."

Gretchen and Miss Granger slowly scanned the juniors first, who would now be seniors. They looked at each picture carefully before turning the page. Next, they looked at the previous year's sophomores, who would now be juniors. Finally, they looked through the freshmen, who comprised this year's sophomore class. "There," Gretchen pointed at a picture. "Glenn Hannity was one of them. If I remember correctly, he was holding my left arm and squeezing my left breast." She and the teacher continued looking through the freshman photos. "Derek Travers. He was the one who led me to the room. And him, Mike Thompson," she added, pointing at a boy a few frames away from Derek. "He was in front trying to pull me toward himself with his hands on my hips. And this boy, Bobbie Wilson, had my right arm and my right breast. Derek was the one behind me who lifted my skirt from behind and reached between my legs to touch my vagina."

Mr. Beck was writing the information on a notebook. "Glenn Hannity, Derek Travers, Mike Thompson, and Bobbie Wilson. You are certain those are the boys who accosted you?"

"Yes," Gretchen answered firmly. "Who knows how far they would have gone if Miss Granger had not stopped them."

Mr. Beck glared at the gym teacher. "Yes, one of the boys' parents has complained about the way Mis Granger intervened. They have said they intend to file a lawsuit against the school district for assault with a deadly weapon."

"They want to sue?" Gretchen asked incredulously. "But their son assaulted me. Miss Granger was just preventing them from hurting me more. She was outnumbered four to one, so she had to use the baseball bat."

The vice principal waved the topic off. "Don't concern yourself with that. It will be in the hands of the attorneys now. What I need to know is how you are going to behave going forward. Will you keep this quiet until the school district's attorneys sort it out? I need your word on this. It could cost us all quite a lot. And the consequences for you would not be good."

Gretchen stared blankly for a moment as his words sunk in. Finally, she spoke. "Yes, I'll keep quiet about it. And Mr. Beck, since this conversation is totally confidential and I know that you will never admit to what we have said here this morning, let me add this.

"Fuck you, Mr. Beck. Fuck you and Parker High and the school district. Fuck you, fuck you, fuck you."

With that, Gretchen gathered up her things, edged her way in front of Miss Granger, and walked out. She heard Mr. Beck shouting in the background, but she ignored him.

16

CHAPTER 16

"Cut the bullshit," Gretchen said angrily. "The mayor just threatened my livelihood because you were seen hanging out with the Russian mob at my press conference. I want to know what his involvement is, and if you are using me to launder dirty money from criminals."

After her speech, she had waited for the City Hall crowd to clear and then hustled Mark into a hidden alcove. The stone tile walls could amplify echoes, so she kept her voice to a loud whisper.

Mark blinked but did not display any outward emotion. Gretchen could not read his expression.

"We are not laundering dirty money, or at least not to my knowledge. The money that I have put into the organization all came from the legitimate income I have received from the racetrack and my other businesses. And the other large donors are in the same situation. They have made large amounts of money, by legitimate means, and they want to support the effort to make San Francisco a shining example again."

"How come I still don't know who the fuck they are? I am the fucking president of this fucking organization, for fuck's sake."

"Take it easy," Mark said with a bit more feeling in his voice this time. "I will give you a full accounting of the donations and where they came from. I assure you, the money is clean."

"Then why were you buddy-buddy with the head of the Russian mob at my press conference?"

Mark blanched slightly. Gretchen wondered if she had hit a nerve. "It had nothing to do with you at all. If you must know, he is trying to muscle in on the racetrack. He was threatening to cause damage if I didn't let his people take over the concessions. And he wants a small percentage of the track's revenue from betting. In as polite of language as I could think of in the heat of the moment, I told him to take a long cylindrical object and apply it with pressure against the opening of his anus."

His description of "shove it" nearly forced a smile to her face, but Gretchen would not allow him to dodge the subject with a gag.

"Why did you take it? You had the mayor not fifty feet away, you had police nearby, you have sheriff's deputies stationed in this building around the clock. Why didn't you turn him in?"

Now Mark put on an expression of fatherly patience. "And what would I say? 'Arrest this man because he said something that hurt my feelings'? And after a few words and mumbled apologies, he would be let go. And later, some of the horses running at our track break their legs on uneven ground and have to be killed. Fans who come to the track might find their tires slashed when they come back out to the parking lot. People who use mayonnaise on our hot dogs might all come down with norovirus and get severely sick, and many more people would start staying away from the track because they think maybe the conditions aren't sanitary. Is that what you would recommend?"

Gretchen found herself on the defensive. "They wouldn't do things like that."

"Correction. *You* wouldn't do things like that, because you don't believe in doing evil things to other people, especially innocent people you have never met. *They*, most assuredly, would do things like that because evil is part of their job description. You are the president of this organization, so you have to stop acting like a naïve little girl. Criminals will absolutely attempt to force you to do things against your will, and they will hurt you, hurt your employees, and hurt the homeless workers you employ in order to get what they want. I am going to protect you from anonymous attacks from my position behind the scenes, but you have to stay sharp. You have to open your eyes and see what people try to do to you. And you have to stay strong enough to kick their asses when they try to hurt you or your people. And kick them hard enough that they are never tempted to try to do it to you again."

Gretchen blinked several times as she absorbed his words. Then she pulled a small notepad and a pen out of her purse.

"Tell me, what were the exact words you used to politely tell that man to shove the fat end of a cue stick up his ass? I may need to learn such terminology and commit it to memory."

17

❧

CHAPTER 17

Gretchen typed her notes of the phone conversation on her iPad, sitting at her desk in the Aurora office. During her lunch break, she had gone downstairs to her The City That Knows How (TCTKH) office to check for messages and found none. Coming back upstairs, she had taken a call from an Aurora client and needed to flesh out her notes while the conversation was fresh in her mind.

She realized she did not often sit in the office when it was empty. As the most sought-after of the ambassadors, Gretchen almost always went out with the others for photo shoots or clients' events. Sometimes she went along primarily to coach the younger members of the crew. While not the oldest woman in the group, she had learned lessons along the way that the others had not, and took them to heart better than any.

But this early afternoon she had the luxury of staying here alone, because she had specifically vetoed her own participation in today's event. Having the place to herself seemed a luxury.

Just before three o'clock, she heard the bus pull up outside, and her colleagues began coming through the ground-floor door. When they got to the top of the stairs and entered the office, Gretchen could almost see grey clouds floating above them, their faces looked so gloomy.

"What happened?" she asked as Melanie sat at her own desk.

"Oh God," Melanie muttered. "I almost wish we had stayed with the

82

Monster Data Mining and the Gorilla Steel lock box bullshit. At least that would have been funny, if not successful. But you were right about that idea that they would respond to this crypto trading company if we said they were building a legacy for their grandchildren. We had a roomful of old people. I mean seventy-five and up. Half of them were either in wheelchairs or using walkers. But they all got excited when we young people started holding their hands and talking about investing."

Gretchen probed gently, seeing that Melanie was already upset. "What happened?"

Melanie choked on her breath, and tears flowed down both of her cheeks. "Gretchen, babe, these were not rich old people. Some of them brought out their bank statements to see how much they could afford to invest, and we could see that these people are on fixed incomes, struggling to get by on Social Security. But they were straining their budgets to try to create investment accounts for their kids, scraping every penny that wasn't already nailed down.

"And Gretchen," she continued, "I looked closely at the terms and conditions in the small print on the forms the investment company is having them sign. Babe, most of these people are never going to see a dime of their money again. And when they die and leave the accounts to their kids, the company is going to impose so many late fees on them that the kids will never get any of it either." Now Melanie was loudly sobbing. "I felt like I was robbing my own blind grandmother, and then kicking her in the shins after I took her money."

Gretchen felt helpless. She reached out and rubbed Melanie's shoulder but could think of nothing to say. Such situations normally called for soothing assurances of, "Don't worry, everything's going to be all right." But she knew better. This so-called investment company was targeting the elderly for a reason. Its executives knew they could easily manipulate seniors, and the victims would not live long enough or raise enough money for attorneys' fees to fight back effectively.

Looking around the office, Gretchen could tell that most of her fellow ambassadors felt the same way. Heidi and Candy approached and put their arms out. Melanie fell into a group hug with them, and all three wept together in each other's arms. Not having been part of the experience at the investment seminar, Gretchen quietly backed out of the cubicle.

She marched straight to Eric's corner office and did not bother knocking. Seeing that the boss was not on the phone or otherwise deeply occupied, she blurted out, "Send everybody home. They need the afternoon off."

Eric looked up wearily. "Not now, Gretchen. It has been a hard afternoon."

"Yes, it has been a hard afternoon. You just sent my colleagues out to commit multiple felonies against people too gullible to defend themselves. Some of them are crying their hearts out right now in the office. Did this client pay the agency in advance?"

Eric shook his head no.

"Then I would recommend that you cancel any invoice you gave them and refuse to accept payment. With or without your permission, I am calling the police to report massive elder financial abuse. How many old people did they have there, and how many do you think signed up to invest?"

Eric looked torn in two. To turn in a client to the police might equal business suicide for him and the Aurora Marketing Agency. On the other hand, the business community might applaud Aurora's integrity, if the news got out. He looked down at his desk for several long moments before finally straightening up and facing her. His eyes still looked tormented, but she sensed determination in his expression.

"You are right." He stood up and walked through the door to stand in the middle of the office. "Everybody, listen up. Gather round please."

The ambassadors stood up from their chairs and stood outside their cubicles, their shoulders sagging. Gretchen did not see a single smiling face among the entire staff.

"Three things," Eric called out in a loud voice. "First, I want you to take the afternoon off and go home. Second, I don't know about you, but I want to take a shower when I get home. I need to wash off all the dirt I feel that I picked up from that investment company today. So, I would suggest that, if you feel the same way, either take a long shower or do something to regain your soul.

"And third—and this is the most important—Aurora is not going to accept any payment from this client. Not a single dime. In fact, I am going to let Gretchen use the phone in my office to call the police and report this investment company for suspected felony criminal activity. She is using my phone so she can close the door against any background noise, but I will give her all the details of today's seminar plus a list of all the victims. If the police come around asking us to sign witness statements, I will sign one and hope that they won't have to involve any of the rest of you. If they do want more of you to sign statements, I will ask for volunteers only. None of you should have to suffer because of this investment company."

"I will sign," Nick called out.

"So will I," yelled Melanie, her eyes still red from tears.

The room erupted in a chorus of shouts of ambassadors willing to sign witness statements. Eric retrieved the list of seniors who had attended the event, and the crew gathered around to add checkmarks next to names on the list identify which ones had enrolled in the company's investment plan, and which ones had already written checks.

Later, armed with facts and details surrounding the event, Gretchen sat down in Eric's office and spread several papers out in order on the desk in front of herself. She had closed the office door, but the entire crew of ambassadors stood outside watching her though the glass wall. Melanie had the palms of her hands against the glass and leaned her forehead against the window as she watched Gretchen intently.

Gretchen picked up the phone and dialed the number she had obtained from the San Francisco Police Department's website.

"Hello, my name is Gretchen Vandella, and I would like the financial crimes unit. I want to report multiple cases of elder financial abuse."

Gretchen spent the next hour on the phone with the police, giving names, addresses, phone numbers and, when possible, dollar amounts. She said she would come to headquarters and sign a formal complaint, but she wanted to report the crimes immediately before the company cashed the checks and the victims lost their money.

Though Eric had told them they could all go home early, the ambassadors did not leave their spots outside the glass wall of Eric's office until Gretchen hung up the phone at the end of an hour. When she opened the door and stepped outside, she was passed from one ambassador to another for a deep hug. When everyone in the crew had gotten a chance to embrace Gretchen, Eric called out, "Well, if none of you are going home, then the first round is on me at Barney's. Hell, the second round too. Let's go."

18

∽

CHAPTER 18

Because Gretchen's name had become a news item with the unveiling of the nonprofit and its mission, an alert reporter for San Francisco's leading daily newspaper took special notice when she saw it while scrolling through police reports. She called it in to the assistant city editor at the paper and got the okay to follow up on it.

At lunchtime Gretchen went downstairs to her TCTKH office to check for messages. Moments later, she reappeared upstairs with a dazed look on her face, and she shuffled across the floor to knock on Eric's door. "We may have a problem."

Eric looked up from his computer screen. "What's up?"

"The *Journal* picked up the police report and wants to interview me."

Eric put one hand on top of his head as if thinking. "Why is that a problem?"

"There is always the possibility of negative publicity. I don't want anything to hurt Aurora. Do you want me to resign to preempt any blowback against the agency?"

Eric motioned toward the guest chair, and Gretchen took a seat. "Let's treat it like any one of our branding projects. What is our goal? What do we want the public to think after this episode has passed? What are the potential actions we can take, and what are the pros and cons of each one of them?"

Gretchen nodded. "Okay scenario number one," she said, taking a sheet of paper and writing it down. "I refuse to return the reporter's call, or I decline to comment or answer her questions. What happens?"

"She writes the story anyway and says Ms. Vandella could not be reached for comment or refused to answer. Either way, the reporter decides how to interpret and report what happened. Could be a plus, could be negative, could be nothing. It all depends on what she has learned from her other sources, and we have absolutely no control or influence over that. In other words, it is a crap shoot."

Gretchen wrote number 2. "I return her call and say that I have separated from Aurora Marketing Agency since this event occurred. What happens?"

Eric replied, "She writes her story with you saying you reported it because the ambassadors told you stories that clearly indicated they had been put into an elder abuse situation without their knowledge and against their will. She starts to think our ambassadors are doing the right thing, but then she asks why you were fired."

"I didn't say I was fired," she snapped.

"You did not say you were not fired, so it is the first obvious conclusion. But if you were not fired, then you suddenly quit. Is it because you no longer wanted to be affiliated with an agency that would engage in crimes like this against vulnerable seniors?"

"Okay, I see where you are going with this. It would make Aurora look terrible." She finished her notation and then wrote number three. "I return her call as a continuing associate of Aurora, answer all of her questions openly and honestly. What happens?"

Eric beamed, "She finds out that our entire crew came back from the client's assignment absolutely devastated, in tears even. The one person who did not go to the assignment was the only one in any condition to collect the facts and call the police. Maybe the Aurora agency should not have accepted this assignment in the first place. But after finding out what it was, in the end the agency did the right thing. It might lose business if potential clients think the agency will turn them in. But the agency would not want clients like that anyway. We come out looking like heroes."

Gretchen was scribbling a few notes. "And what do we think of this person who called the police? Was she just grandstanding?"

"She is the biggest hero of all," Eric says firmly. "She didn't go on the assignment because she thought the investment company smelled fishy. When her coworkers came back in tears, she took action immediately. And this is the woman who's going to clean up our city."

"Yikes, I had forgotten about that," Gretchen said. "Do you think I should call Mark Fischer to warn him?"

Eric only hesitated for a moment. "Ordinarily I would say yes. But that would be tantamount to giving him possible veto power over a decision that primarily affects my company, not his. Maybe you should talk to the reporter first, then call Mark afterward. That way, you will be able to tell him how the interview went and what direction the story will most likely take. But you will not give him the power to stop you from doing it, because you will have already done it."

Gretchen finished her notes and then got up to leave. "Yeah, I think you are right. I hope this doesn't blow up in my face. I am kind of enjoying this side gig, and it is just now starting to get off the ground."

Eric held up one hand to stop her. "Wait a minute. You did the right thing. Don't you ever be ashamed of doing the right thing. You may have saved all those old people from losing their savings. I am proud of you. And maybe the other ambassadors out there in the office haven't come right out and told you to your face yet, but they are all proud of you too. You were on the phone, so you could not hear what they were saying outside this room in the main office. They are one hundred percent behind you, and so am I. If we take a hit for this, so be it. But we will take the hit with our heads held high."

Gretchen smiled grimly and gave a mock salute. "'Tis a far, far better thing that I do than I have ever done before," paraphrasing a line she remembered from her childhood spoken by a character about to be executed.

19

CHAPTER 19

Gretchen finished reading the last page of the report from the non-profit organization that was handling hiring and supervision of workers. The cleanup campaign would start with just 100 workers concentrated in the downtown, South-of-Market, Upper Market, and the Fisherman's Wharf areas. The organization would devote several of its own staff members to supervise the street workers. Those street workers selected for this first wave had already given their names, Social Security numbers, and other identifying information. All were homeless, so they could not give addresses. All would be paid daily by check, and, because they could not be expected to have bank accounts, their supervisors would have them endorse the checks at the end of the day and would cash the checks for them on the spot. After a week of receiving daily pay, the agency would transition the workers to weekly paychecks and would attempt to get them into single-room-occupancy hotels in the Tenderloin, South-of-Market, and other areas. People who had never faced housing problems considered the SRO hotels as flophouses, but to some of the homeless they would be like resorts. Residents needed to share bathrooms on each floor, but the relatively low rent would put the rooms within reach.

The workers would start their jobs tomorrow morning. Gretchen had not considered herself religious since her early teens, but she said a prayer now.

Glancing at the desk clock, she realized she had stayed in her office much later than planned. She needed to get home and sleep. Tomorrow would demand that she make appearances in several high-profile areas. She would pose with Senator Grady in the financial district, with the mayor at the foot of Market Street with the Ferry Building tower in the background, and with three members of the Board of Supervisors at locations in their home districts.

It would be a long day. She was about to turn off her desk lamp when the desk phone rang.

"Is your computer on?" Eric asked when she answered. "Go to the *Journal's* website and pull up the front page."

She typed the URL into the browser and clicked the Return key.

"Oh my God, that picture is from the press conference."

"Yes," Eric said, "but the story is about the police report. When the story jumps to page ten, there's a sidebar story about your campaign to clean up the city. Between the two stories, you have got half the front page and all of page ten."

"I haven't been able to read it yet. Is any of it negative?"

Eric chuckled. "Baby Girl, I don't think so. Of course, you never know if somebody is going to get envious of the publicity and lash out at you in jealousy. But I think you are going to be seen as a champion tomorrow morning."

"How about the agency?"

"Aurora? We turned down payment for an assignment that we decided was dishonest. And though we have never advertised ourselves or what we do in the field of marketing, our name is out there now. I think we are going to come out okay."

Gretchen took a moment to collect herself. "So, this story hits the streets tomorrow morning. Oh my God," she said, "I just remembered that tomorrow morning is the beginning of the cleanup campaign. I am supposed to pose for pictures with the mayor and the senator and some other people. I had better call Mark and warn him what is coming, and the potential for it to blow up."

Eric chuckled again. "Baby Girl, read the stories before you call him. I think you will be pleased."

* * *

"Mark, are you in a comfortable place?"

"Yes, why?"

"Have a seat, please. The *Journal* is running a story with a photo of me on the front page tomorrow morning, just as we are about to start the cleanup campaign."

"That's wonderful—"

"Slow down. We don't know what the reaction is going to be." Gretchen then outlined what had happened with the crypto trading company investment scheme. "The front-page story is me accusing this company of trying to bilk elderly seniors out of their savings. The story about the cleanup campaign is on page ten, next to the continuation of the investment article. It could cast the campaign in a negative light. Or if you really are arguing with the Russian mob, it could ignite a war if they connect me to you."

Mark hushed her. "Don't worry about me. I want to know how you are holding up. You are more important."

Gretchen caught a lump in her throat but recovered quickly. "Why, thank you for worrying about me. That means a lot to me. It really does."

"Certainly, you must know I care for you a lot."

"Um," she stammered, "I really wasn't sure."

"I admire you a great deal, and I have high respect for the work you do," he said. "So put that out of your mind. Now, as for dealing with this unexpected publicity, are you fearful for your own safety?"

"No, I am probably more worried about how it will affect Aurora and The City That Knows How. And of course, as a result of that, what impact it will have on my career."

Mark kept silent on his end of the line for a long space, then he spoke more softly than his usual forthright, commanding tone. "Gretchen, it is only nine fifteen. Can I meet you for a drink, or do you need to go to sleep soon? I am at the hotel in Half Moon Bay again, so I could slip up to Pacifica in a few minutes if that works for you."

She stopped to consider the possibilities. She could drive to the Dew Drop Inn in just a few minutes. Not the sort of place a billionaire would ordinarily frequent, but he was a racetrack owner and probably knew the Dew Drop Inn's type of clientele very well. Or would it be too forward to invite him to her condo? Gretchen tried to weigh the pros and cons of both options. In a flash of intuition, as the newspaper story reared its head again, she made a decision and gave him directions to the Dew Drop Inn. "I warn you. It is a dive bar. But I do not think it would be very crowded tonight, so your identity and reputation would probably stay intact."

Mark laughed and said he would see her after the short drive up the coast highway.

Gretchen cast a wary eye at herself in the mirror. She looked okay, but not good enough for a client, especially one who was paying her a huge ten thousand dollars a week and giving her a huge operating budget to run a huge program on a huge gamble. She quickly added some highlight on her cheekbones and rouge on the cheeks. She would apply fresh lipstick when she parked her car at the bar. She ran her brush through her hair once, satisfied that it looked good. She applied just a hint of scent to her wrists.

She had no problem parking her car, because only three spaces at the bar had cars in them. She recognized the sports car as Mark's. Inside the dark tavern, she waved to Bob, the bartender, who had worked there for as long as Gretchen had been old enough to drink legally, and probably much longer than that. Mark sat at a table in the corner.

"What are you drinking?" she asked without sitting down. "They don't have waitresses here to take your order, and you won't find any little umbrellas in your glass."

At the bar, she asked Bob for a Johnny Walker Black double on ice, and a glass of Zin for herself. "I will start a tab," she said, as she wrapped the glasses in a pair of paper napkins and carried them to the table.

"I must say that the servers here are beautiful," Mark commented with a grin.

"Thank you, sir, and you can tuck my tips into my waistband," Gretchen joked. Taking her seat, she decided to be bold. "Seriously, I think that's the first time you have said anything about my appearance. And since I make my living off my looks, that had me very worried."

He watched her intently over the rim of his glass as he took a sip of his whiskey. Setting the glass down, he smiled warily. "I am an employer of a large number of people, so my human resources department has made me intensely aware of how harmful sexual harassment can be, both to the recipients of the harassment and the employer, whether it is intentional or not. It is not just that I don't want to be sued by an employee. More importantly, I don't want to damage the working relationship I have with that person, because that could limit the creativity she might put into her work. Of course," he said, looking into her eyes, "it is totally different if it is all consensual. But in an employer and employee relationship, it is always assumed the employer is dominant and the aggressor."

She also looked at him over the rim of her glass. "Fortunately, I am not an employee. I am the president of The City That Knows How. You happen to be a benefactor, a very generous one at that. But you are not part of my organization."

Mark laughed loud and long, straight from the gut. He started to take another sip of his drink but thought better of it as another wave of laughter erupted from his chest. He smacked his hand down on the table to punctuate the final titter, and then spoke.

"You said a minute ago that you make your living off of your looks. Yes, you are beautiful. But you already know that, and you don't need me to tell you. I chose to ask you if you wanted to take on this role because of your mind. You stood out in the crowd at that event for the racetrack, so I did some research. Your face could launch a thousand ships. But your wit and wisdom could prevent the war in the first place so that launching the ships would not be necessary."

Gretchen made a show of batting her eyelashes like a schoolgirl in an exaggerated fashion.

"Why, I don't think anyone has ever paid me a compliment like that, sir. Flattery will get you everywhere." She took another sip of her wine. "But let me be serious here for a minute. This story in the *Journal* tomorrow could blow up in our faces. If the public finds out that I am a brand ambassador who essentially makes her living by manipulating people's emotions, then the cleanup campaign might look phony. If they think I attacked the crypto investment company just to generate publicity for the campaign, then both of them might look phony. If they think organized crime is involved in any way, they might think the whole thing is just a money-laundering scheme."

Mark cut her off. "And if they just look at your face in the pictures, they might fall in love. And if they see homeless people out cleaning up the streets and earning an honest wage, they might love you more. And those politicians that want to have their pictures taken with you? They are hoping that some of that love will rub off on them."

He reached across to place his hand over hers on the tabletop. "Do not second-guess yourself, my friend. I think you are brilliant. And I think you are going to have a fantastic day. I believe in you."

She squeezed his hand, and then drained her glass. "Speaking of tomorrow, I should probably get out of here."

Mark paid Bob, and the two of them went out to the parking lot together. Mark accompanied Gretchen to her car and stood behind her while she unlocked the driver's door. She turned to him to say goodnight. She had never felt closer to him. In fact, in that moment she realized she had not felt this close to any man for years, not since that terrible incident when she was a sixteen-year-old high school student. In the years since then, she had learned to manipulate men with her body and her words, but she had built a wall around herself. She could venture out, but nobody could come in. It was safer that way. She had been safe for years.

Suddenly, Gretchen leaned forward and tilted her head upward. She gently pressed her lips against Mark's, and then pulled back slightly. Mark put both of his hands against the small of her back and pushed his lips against hers with passion. Their tongues slithered over each other in a flurry of passion, and Gretchen could hear his breath quicken even as her heart thumped against her ribs.

"Would you like to come to my hotel?" he asked.

"I have appearances scheduled in the morning. Follow me to my place."

* * *

When she closed her front door behind them, Mark pulled her into his arms for a long, deep kiss. Caught up in the moment, she began untucking and unbuttoning his shirt, trying to yank it off of his shoulders. She began pulling him toward her bedroom, kicking off her shoes and shedding her blouse along the way. They could not keep their mouths apart as they tried to strip. Gretchen discovered that Mark's chest and arms seemed solid with muscle. She grabbed the waistband of his shorts and pushed them down over his hips. She let her own panties drop to the floor and stepped out of them.

Gretchen pulled the cover back on her bed, and the two of them tumbled onto the sheets together. After rubbing, caressing, and licking each other's chests and stomachs, Gretchen started to move her mouth down toward his midsection.

"Whoa," he said, pulling her back. He laid her down on her back, kissed and licked her breasts, and then playfully ran his tongue down the length of her stomach. "There is an unwritten law among gentlemen: The lady always comes first. At least once. Twice is better," he added as he dipped his mouth between her legs.

Gretchen shivered at the sensation, which had been missing from her life for longer than she could remember. "Mmmm," she moaned, "other men I have known seemed unaware of that law."

"They," Mark said, raising his head from his ministrations, "were not gentlemen."

* * *

Gretchen woke up early, though she had not nodded off until well after two in the morning. Despite the short hours of sleep, she felt refreshed and energetic. She swung her legs off the mattress to get up and smiled at the soreness she felt below the waist, both in front and in back. But it was a good soreness, like the ache of stretched muscles after a good workout at the gym. Ah, she wondered how many calories she had burned off in her long session of lovemaking with Mark. Looking over her shoulder in the mirror, she was almost surprised that there was no redness on the cheek of her butt. But she could still remember the surprisingly exciting sting that she felt when he spanked her in throes of the moment. She grinned at herself in the mirror like a schoolgirl who had just gotten her first kiss.

Mark had gone back to his hotel after their lovemaking. True to his word, he observed his "unwritten rule among gentlemen." She had reached her peak not once, not twice, but several times. Now, with a busy morning ahead of her, Gretchen put freshly roasted coffee beans into her grinder, and after running it for ten seconds, poured the grounds into her coffee maker. She put an English muffin in the toaster oven, and then went to the bathroom to take a quick shower.

Wrapping her head in a towel afterward, she put marmalade on one half of her muffin, and a thin layer of cream cheese on the other half. Before sitting down to eat, she glanced at her answering machine and saw the red light flashing. A call must have come in while she was showering. As she was about to press the play button, the number next to the flashing light registered in her mind. No, it was more than one call.

"Hey, Gretchen, this is Heidi. You have got to pick up today's newspaper. See you at the office tomorrow." The machine clicked to the next message.

"Gretchen, Eric here. My phone has been ringing off the hook since the sun came up. It is all good so far."

"Ms. Vandella, this is Linda Hope at television station KICU. If you are available, I would like to interview you on camera about the growing problem of elder financial abuse. Specifically, scam artists who target vulnerable seniors. Please call me at four, one, five, three, oh, nine, one, six, oh, four."

"Ms. Vandella, this is Mayor Blum's office. He was hoping you could arrive fifteen minutes earlier at the photo shoot at the foot of Market. He would like a few minutes to speak to you privately."

Gretchen went to her closet to select an outfit both businesslike and feminine. And a scarf. A colorful scarf should go over the whole ensemble.

20

CHAPTER 20

"I am so proud to be here with this bright young woman to launch our new campaign to clean up the streets of San Francisco," the mayor almost shouted into the microphone on the podium that had been set up. In their quick meeting before the scheduled event, the mayor had explained to Gretchen that, in order to capitalize on the unexpected publicity, his office had arranged for the public works director, the administrator for homeless programs, and several other department heads to join them and make brief statements praising the initiative. Gretchen quickly made calls to the offices of the other dignitaries she was supposed to make appearances with today to warn them that she might be a bit late for their scheduled joint appearances.

"And I am especially proud," the mayor continued, "because we have learned this morning that this young woman, Gretchen Vandella, is also a fierce warrior defending vulnerable senior citizens. Now, these are only allegations of wrongdoing at this time, so the accused will still have their day in court. But it is true that a number of our most vulnerable senior citizens were about to sign away their life savings on an investment that warrants closer scrutiny. In a few minutes, I would like to introduce our district attorney to describe what Ms. Vandella uncovered and what the police investigators are going to be looking into. But first, let me give you the director of public works to describe to you how The City That Knows How is going to put San Francisco back on track."

Several more speakers came to the podium over the course of the next thirty minutes. Finally, Gretchen herself was given the chance to speak. However, knowing that it would be best to keep it short so the TV crews could edit their videos and get the story onto the air as soon as possible, she spoke for less than five minutes and tried to incorporate several key phrases that would work well as sound bites on brief clips. As the crews wrapped up, reporters asked her to answer a few questions away from the podium. The mayor climbed into his limousine and left.

Gretchen connected with Linda Hope, the reporter from KICU, and quietly arranged to get together with her and her cameraman around the corner, out of sight of the other crews that were at that moment narrating their stories in front of their cameras. Speaking briefly, she outlined why she had grown suspicious of the investment company's rules of operation, and this led her to refuse to participate in the company's seminar. And she grew dramatic when she described the horror her coworkers felt when they found out what the company was asking the elderly investors to sign, and how many of them were in tears when they returned to the office. Finally, she described how the head of Aurora had called the company and told them he was refusing payment and would decline any future business with them.

"We are what the marketing industry calls brand ambassadors," Gretchen explained. "We examine a client's brand—what it is that they stand for—and if we support it, we will help explain it to the public. But when my coworkers discovered what they were being asked to explain, some of them felt physically ill. One of them told me she felt like she had been asked to beat her own grandmother with a bat."

Gretchen did not say more, because she saw Linda nod to her cameraman. They would seize on that last remark as the primary soundbite for the story. The rest of the details would be available for those who wanted them, but the reporter was looking for something that would take less than ten or fifteen seconds of airtime. Coworkers feeling physically ill as if they were beating their grandmothers—that was it.

Gretchen hailed a taxi and rode to her next appearance.

The afternoon passed with a flurry of similar, but much shorter, events with some members of the Board of Supervisors whose districts were most heavily impacted by unclean streets and high concentrations of homeless people. Local neighborhood news outlet reporters appeared at these stops and asked questions specific to their neighborhood concerns. These stories would mostly show up on the front pages of weekly or monthly papers that were thrown on residents' front porches for free. While far less influential than the daily paper or the broadcast stations, these throwaways nevertheless reinforced popular news trends for retirees and other stay-at-home residents.

After the third neighborhood appearance, Gretchen caught a cab back to the office.

21

CHAPTER 21

The phone rang almost as soon as Gretchen hung up the previous call. The constant demand for her attention had continued for seven days now. Fortunately, Eric had only scheduled her for one shoot this week, and for photos only, not any speaking parts or mingling at a social event. She had worked in her tiny office on the ground floor almost full-time each day. The nonprofit handling the hiring, supervision, and payroll was keeping the street-cleaning project running, so that did not require much time from her. But a legion of elderly people who had been scammed by con artists were calling and begging for help. She could only listen to their stories and express sympathy, and take down their names and numbers. Inwardly, she had no idea if she would ever be able to do anything for any of these people. But they seemed to take comfort that she listened to them. Several had told her that the worst part of their situation was that no one would listen to them.

But it left her no time for anything else. Eric made allowances, so her occasional absences from Aurora had not yet put a strain on their working relationship. And Aurora had gotten so much favorable publicity from the elder financial abuse story that several large new clients had signed on with the agency.

She picked up the phone and dialed upstairs. "Hey, Boss, how are you today?"

He laughed. "You are still calling me Boss? Well, babe, things are great. What can I do ya for?"

"I need to talk. Do you want to do it here, or should I come to your office? Or would you like to go somewhere and let me buy you a cup of coffee?"

"Wow, this must be serious." He pondered for a moment. "Let's get out of here. Coffee or a drink?"

They decided to slip into Barney's. She had her new favorite, red Zinfandel wine from Amador County in the Sierra foothills, while he ordered a pint of the bar's own craft-brewed beer. Seeing only a few other customers in the place, they felt comfortable sitting at the bar.

"I am thinking about offering some ambassadors a bit of part-time work, if that's okay with you." She outlined the sudden spike in activity that was overwhelming her. "I have only been doing this for a week, and already I need to set up a bureaucracy to support it. I was tempted to put in a multi-tiered voicemail system—'To report a case of elder financial abuse, please press two'—but these old people really want to talk to a live human being. They want to think somebody is paying attention to them, and a voicemail system just won't cut it. I need somebody to help handle the calls."

Eric looked sympathetic. "My poor Baby Girl. You need to off-load some of this stuff. Now, the elder abuse calls are somewhat related to Aurora, because we were the ones who had the trading company account. Now it has taken on a life of its own. Do you want to keep it for The City That Knows How, or do you want somebody outside to take it over? I am not sure if the Aurora Agency can do it, unless it becomes so big of a cause that a client pays us to handle it."

"I know," Gretchen said. "That's why I was thinking of offering a few of the ladies some part-time pay to handle those calls. Or I could just hire a receptionist to answer the phones."

"Who on our crew were you thinking of?"

She stopped to think for a moment. "Somebody who's hungry, who needs the extra money. Several people on a rotational schedule, because it could take over a single person's entire day. What do you think of

Stephanie? And Melanie? Melanie prompted this whole concern when she started crying in the office after that investment seminar."

Eric nodded. "Would two be enough? Nick is the one who first told us it could be a federal offense. And having one man might help."

Gretchen drained her glass. "Three would give me a big boost. I will approach them privately and offer them only what I am paying the homeless to clean up the streets, double the minimum wage. If I paid too much, they would get comfortable spending a lot of time on it. I don't want to take them away from their ambassador work."

Eric also finished his beer and prepared to leave. "Good. By the way, how are things with Mark Fischer?"

Gretchen blushed. "Um, very good, actually."

He laughed when he saw her sheepish grin and suddenly reddening cheeks. "My Baby Girl! You go, girl."

22

CHAPTER 22

The woman held the steam pressure washer hose while her male partner made adjustments on the control panel of the unit. Gretchen and a dozen members of a downtown business association watched approvingly as the woman washed hardened globs of stuck-on chewing gum and other grime off the sidewalk. Five of Aurora's ambassadors mixed in with the group, commenting that they were pleased that they did not see trash on the ground in this area anymore. The business association's newsletter editor took pictures and recorded comments to put into an article later.

One of the association members had just told Gretchen about a compliment he had gotten from a visiting out-of-town client when something caught Gretchen's eye. She happened to glance toward a man standing near the signal at the far end of the block. It was Mark. Though happy to see him, she wondered what had brought him here today. They planned to meet for dinner, but he had said nothing about coming downtown today.

Excusing herself from the group, she stepped off the curb to go around the sidewalk washers and then walked down the block to the corner. She and Mark stood near enough to hear each other but did not give outward signs of addressing each other.

"What brings you here today?"

Mark kept a broad smile on his face as he looked about, but his voice carried a tone of worry. "Keep a tight watch on your workers today. We might have trouble."

Gretchen also kept a smile in case anyone was watching. "How so? Russians?"

"Far worse. American-born, home-grown gangs. I got word they're going to try to rob your workers after they get paid tonight. So, I am putting guards at every one of your pay stations."

Still smiling, she asked, "Uniformed guards?"

Now he turned at looked at her face. "No. You won't even know they are there. Neither will the gangs, unless they make a move against your workers. If they do, my people will make an example of them. An example that all the other will see and hear about."

Nodding farewell, Mark started to turn. "Are we still on for dinner?"

"Absolutely." Gretchen stood alone at the corner for a few more minutes observing the activity on the street, in case anyone had seen her near Mark and might connect the two of them. Then she strolled back up the street to the group observing the sidewalk washers. The work was proceeding more quickly now.

"Tell me," said the newsletter editor, "do you have just this one steam pressure cleaner, or are there others? This is all very nice, but we have many hundreds of city blocks to worry about."

"Yes, hundreds of blocks just here in the financial district alone," Gretchen agreed. "We are currently renting ten of these units to spread out across the problem areas. Later, as contributors' donations build up our operating budget, we will increase the number of cleaners and start buying rather than renting the machines. We are looking at warehouse space in the South-of-Market to store the equipment, and we will hire homeless people with administrative skills to manage that warehousing facility."

She rattled off some figures almost without thinking about them. Meanwhile, however, after hearing Mark's warning, she peered at anyone and everyone nearby. She suddenly felt suspicious of passersby, of people standing at the bus stop across the street, of anyone whose face might be visible in an office window on an upper floor of the surrounding buildings. Who knew which of those people might be watching her on behalf of some street gang intent on robbing her workers? Who knew if they were taking photographs, marking down patterns of behavior, taking note of who talked to whom? Gretchen had never felt such an intense wave of paranoia before. Mark's warning suddenly made the entire world look potentially hostile. Would she ever trust a new acquaintance as innocent again?

The steam cleaning demonstration concluded, and the businesspeople left. Gretchen nodded subtly to the ambassadors as they each walked away in different directions, not wishing to tip off observers that they came as parts of a group. She was especially glad now, in light of Mark's revelation, that as a matter of course the team always avoided looking like a team at social events. If organized crime was watching, she certainly would not want any threats made against the Aurora Marketing Agency or its ambassadors. It was bad enough that she had to worry about her own safety now. How much worse if she needed to watch out for her coworkers too.

She had planned to go back to the office, but now she felt she could not dare to abandon the payroll crew. They would be dispensing and cashing checks for the workers in an hour and a half, so she decided to duck into a coffeeshop to camp out with a cup of dark roast and her cell phone.

"Eric," she said into the phone as a waitress brought a piece of cherry pie and refilled her cup. "Heads up. Mark says gangs are threatening to rob my street workers after they get paid tonight. Our ambassadors have already left, but make sure nobody from the office comes back down here this afternoon."

"Oh my God, Gretchen. Are you okay? Do you want me to come pick you up?"

"No, I am going to stay with the payroll crew at Hallidie Plaza. Mark says he is going to have people guarding us. I think they're going to protect the workers too. But I don't want any Aurora ambassadors down here, because I don't know if he has enough people to protect them too."

"But what about you? Are you going to be safe?"

"Yeah, Eric, I think I will probably be okay. Mark and I are supposed to be meeting for dinner. If he is got an army of people protecting my workers, he probably told them to keep an eye out for me too."

Eric chuckled. "Meeting for dinner again? My Baby Girl!"

"Oh, stop," she sputtered. "I am running a side business now, so I have to go to business meetings."

"Yes, dear, if that's what you want to call it."

"Goodnight, Eric. Go find somebody else to tease."

* * *

The payroll operation operated out of a booth in the transit plaza at the Powell Street Station on Market Street. The plaza was outside the exit from the underground station for the city and Bay Area subway systems and opened to view from the street level above. The workers from the downtown financial district, South of Market, and Upper Market could all get to this location easily. And with the cable car turnaround and department stores in the area, the area was public enough to discourage theft. Still, as she stood adjacent to the booth where workers were lined up to endorse their checks in exchange for cash, Gretchen anxiously looked this way and that, and scanned the safety rails on the street level above to see if anyone was watching.

She saw no one who looked suspicious, which made it only worse. Now she suspected everyone. It could be any of these seemingly innocent bystanders. And where were Mark's people? He had promised her that he would have somebody guarding them. Oh wait—did he say that she would not see them, that she would remain unaware of their presence? But if she was unaware, then the gangs would be unaware too. They would have no reason not to attack. What good were guards if the bad guys were not scared off and attacked anyway?

The payroll crew and workers continued, blissfully unaware of the danger that might be looking down at them from the street above. The men and women who had been collecting and disposing of trash, steam cleaning sidewalks, and staffing the warehouse chatted among themselves in line. When each reached the front, he or she would show an i.d. card and would receive a check. Only a very few had their own checking accounts; the rest would endorse their checks and let the payroll people cash them. Gretchen watched to make sure they folded up their money and put it in their wallets or pockets before going upstairs to the street level. No need to make targets of themselves by flashing cash openly.

The workers had formed three lines for the three payroll workers, so the entire operation finished in half an hour. They packed up the paperwork and folded up their table and chairs. Several of the workers stayed to help carry the gear upstairs where a van would pull up to a curb when everything was ready. In this neighborhood, the van would not attempt to park at the curb more than a minute or two. The city considered parking tickets as a major source of revenue, and parking control officers would pounce on the van if it lingered.

Gretchen went up to the street level and was surprised to see three sets of flashing red lights. One came from an ambulance across the street at the corner of Fifth and Market, where paramedics were lifting a man on a gurney. Another ambulance was parked above the transit plaza on Mason Street, but she could not see what the paramedics were doing there. And immediately in front of the cable car turnaround, a police car had stopped at the curb on Market Street. One officer was putting a zip tie on the wrists of a man lying face down on the sidewalk, while a second officer stood close by talking to a woman whom Gretchen recognized at one of her sidewalk steam washers. The woman waved at Gretchen, so she approached.

"Miss Gretchen, a man tried to rob me," the worker said.

"Oh my God, I am so sorry that happened to you. Officer, what is happening here now?" Gretchen asked.

The cop looked at her and apparently recognized her from the newspaper pictures. "You are the person who manages the cleanup, aren't you? Well, this guy," he said, indicating the one the other officer was now lifting to his feet, "tried to take the cash that this woman had just received."

"But you were here to stop him."

"No, not us," he said. "Apparently, your program is so popular that somebody out here on the street saw what was happening and stepped forward to stop it. By the time we got here, this guy was already on the ground, barely conscious. The woman here had stayed behind to tell us what happened, but whoever it was that came to her rescue was already gone."

The policeman laughed and pointed at the two ambulances. "Same thing happened over there. Somebody was trying to rob your workers, but ordinary citizens stepped forward to stop them. Our guy here got off lucky—at least he can walk. The other two will be booked in the police ward at San Francisco General Hospital. I tell you, I have never seen anything like this. Your program is so popular that regular citizens are stepping forward to get involved, stepping forward to protect the workers. Of course, I wish they would just hold the criminals until we arrive to arrest them properly instead of beating them to a pulp and leaving them in a heap on the ground. But still, it is just amazing." The policeman's grin made Gretchen suspect that, though he said he wished the robbers had not been beaten, he was just saying so for the record. His grin suggested he fully supported the turn of events as they had occurred.

Gretchen allowed herself a smile in response but struggled to avoid laughing out loud. If the police put out the story that ordinary citizens were stepping forward to protect the workers, so much the better. It would generate good publicity. But she could guess what had really happened.

* * *

"That's very interesting," Mark said blandly as he buttered a dinner roll. "That regular people would get involved like that. Do you see the new sense of civic pride that you have created?"

Gretchen snickered. Tonight, she was drinking Cabernet Sauvignon, fruity but not as sweet as Zin. She had just started her second glass, but after today did not worry that she was drinking on an empty stomach. Still, to play it safe, she also took a bread roll from the basket and cut a sliver of it.

"Mark Fischer, you know as well as I that it wasn't regular citizens who stepped forward out of civic pride," she said with a grin. "Now I am wondering what sort of man I have taken up with. You seem to have an army of urban guerillas at your disposal."

He raised his eyebrows in innocence. "Who, me? I don't know what you are talking about. I am just a simple country boy from a horse farm in Kentucky. Regular people out in the country step forward to protect their neighbors when somebody tries to get rough. I am so happy to learn that they do it here in the big city too."

Gretchen nibbled at her bread. "I don't know whether to praise you for protecting my people or to turn you in to the police for running a gang of vigilantes."

"How about you just thank me for my efforts to support The City That Knows How? I will have you know that the head of a local foundation told me today it is considering donating half a million dollars to the organization. And this foundation wants publicity for its good works, so it will let us attach its name to the donation when the press and the mayor's staff ask."

Gretchen had stopped her wine glass halfway to her mouth. "Half a million?"

"Yep. Based almost entirely on your appearances with the mayor and other dignitaries but also heavily influenced by your noble quest to defend vulnerable senior citizens. I think you should wear a cape at your next press conference."

After dinner, she accompanied him to his hotel. Anticipating this decision, she had packed an overnight bag with a change of clothes. And a jar of flavoring, a vial of scented oil, and a tube of lubricant.

23

***

CHAPTER 23

The reporter on the phone had asked the same question four different ways, in what Gretchen recognized as journalists' method to coax a revelation, a contradiction, or a more forceful declaration out of a reluctant source. In this particular case, Gretchen would not fall for it because the results could cause danger, even physical harm for some people. So, she patiently laid out her position again.

In the wake of the attempted payroll robberies and the subsequent attacks, the issue of taking back the streets by force had come to dominate the news. Several neighborhood safety groups had left voicemail messages asking Gretchen to come speak at their community meetings, but she had not yet returned their calls.

"I do not support vigilantism, and I abhor violence," she said into the phone. "If normal citizens are stepping forward to protect the homeless workers who are cleaning up our streets, then I am proud of them and I am proud of the new civic pride taking hold here in San Francisco. But I wish they could just cooperate with the police to nab the suspects, not beat them to within an inch of their lives. Violence is never the right answer."

The reporter wouldn't let go. "But isn't it necessary to operate outside the law sometimes to get things done? After all, your street-cleaning program is not a government operation. You saw a need and took action, without waiting for the government to give permission. Isn't that what The City That Knows How is all about?"

This sort of question had been dogging Gretchen for weeks now. She knew quite well that the news industry was built on highlighting conflicts in opinions, disagreements on methods, variations on traditional approaches. Reporters would seize on any minor change of course to inflate the sense of divergence from the past, to make it look like there was a fight brewing over a message or method. It made for headlines, and headlines sold more newspapers, and the increased circulation for the newspapers sold the advertising that supported the news industry.

"Look," she said, "We created a non-profit organization through the government's rules. This allows donors to make donations that they can deduct on their tax returns, again working through government rules. Our cleanup program worked with the city to make sure we did not interfere with government programs, that we did not break any government rules.

"And on another topic, when I saw what I suspected was financial abuse of vulnerable senior citizens, I did not go kick the asses of the executives at the investment company. I called the police and let them initiate a proper investigation. I did not take justice into my own hands. And I do not want vigilantes doing that to people on the street either."

The reporter baited her. "But a lot of people say you did kick those executives' asses."

"Not true," was all she could say. "I recognized what I thought was a problem, and I reported it to the appropriate authorities."

The reporter switched to a different line of questioning. "So, what is in the future for the program?"

Glad to get away from the personal side, Gretchen launched into a rehearsed response. "First, we will continue expanding into other parts of the city. We want all the neighborhoods to look and feel cleaner and healthier. And we will continue helping our workers get into housing, so they don't have to sleep on the streets. We will try to help them develop their other skills so they can get jobs in the fields they worked in before they lost their homes. This could take a long time, so we have our work cut out for us."

* * *

After hanging up, she straightened the papers on her desk, left the office and locked the door, and went upstairs to her cubicle in the Aurora office. All the ambassadors had their heads down as they studied folders of material spread out on their desks. No sounds of conversation interfered with the relative silence in the room. Eric saw her enter and motioned her over to his office.

"What's up, Boss? It looks like everybody is studying for their final exam or something out there."

He handed Gretchen a folder that looked like what her coworkers were studying. "All hands on deck for this one, babe. We got a major local clothing manufacturer signing on for a change in image. They want to project a casual line separate from their more elegant attire."

She scanned through the pages of the material without stopping to read the details. Silk Industries, the parent company, had a long-established brand that simply oozed wealth and taste, but the illustrations and charts of data on these pages all pointed to the mass market. The top of the line here would just barely reach the level of Smart Casual in Aurora's dressing room.

"Okay," she said. "I will study the data. We have got population figures, market share, manufacturing capacity, cycles of mid-market fashion trend cycles over the past twenty-five years, projections of trends for the next ten years. They are clearly making a major shift in their brand and marketing strategy for the long term.

"So, what prompted the change?"

Eric grinned. "The homeless. The company thinks the homeless are going be getting into permanent housing in the next decade, and they're going to need clothes. Nothing fancy, but well-made and manufactured here in the United States instead of overseas. They want to position themselves for the market when it emerges."

"Okay, that makes sense.," Gretchen still didn't look convinced. "But they have a national company with an international market. Their headquarters occupies a prestigious building on Wilshire Boulevard in Los Angeles. How did they happen to choose the Aurora Marketing Agency four hundred miles north in San Francisco?"

Eric's grin widened. "They decided they needed some strategizing from outside L.A. Like maybe from the city that knows how."

She stared, waiting for him to elaborate. When he did not, she asked, "As in the description of San Francisco?"

"Well, that too. But primarily as in the name of the organization."

She slapped the folder down on his desk. "You are kidding me."

Eric held up his hand slightly. "Don't let it go to your head. They've been planning this marketing move for more than a year. But you happened to hit the news just before they were ready to go public. So, they want to ride your organization's coattails."

"What is our assignment?"

"We are working a shareholders' conference in Los Angeles in two weeks. Not a fashion show, they are holding a conference where the top speaker will be a senior trade official from the federal government. We expect that he will be emphasizing the need to do more domestic manufacturing. You already know that only two percent of the clothing worn in America is manufactured in America. Most of it comes from sweatshops overseas. This company, Silk Industries, already makes its clothing domestically in the U.S., so it thinks it should corner a bigger part of the market quickly."

Gretchen's eyes seemed to be gazing into the distance, even though she sat in the cramped confines of Eric's office. "Hmm. Do you happen to know how much they pay their garment workers?"

Eric furrowed his brows. "Not off the top of my head. Why do you ask?"

"I was wondering. For this clothing line for the masses, as opposed to their usual lines for the wealthy, do you think they'd be willing to pay their workers twice the national minimum wage?"

He snapped his finger. "The same that you are paying the homeless to clean up the streets?"

"Exactly. If they want to tie their marketing to our movement, they should go all the way in. And if they think the formerly homeless will make up their new customer base, this will help grow that base for them. They will not only be making a fashion statement. It would be a political statement that says they identify with the struggles of the lower classes. The wash-and-wear crowd has probably never even heard of Silk Industries before, but this would make them a topic of conversation. And from there, it would not only be a topic but also a source for the people's new clothing. And it will be made in America."

Eric put his elbow on his desk and rested his chin on the knuckles of his left hand while he considered the notion. He jotted a few notes with his right hand on a pad of paper and looked at his thoughts on paper.

"Would you be able to join me for a video conference with their senior officers in a few days?"

"Of course," she answered. "What are you thinking?"

"Our whole crew will be serving as ambassadors at this shareholders meeting. They had raised the possibility of elevating one member of the group to the star status, the most visible ambassador of the group. They did not specify who they wanted, but it sounded like they were thinking of somebody like Candy. You know—boobs, hips, blonde hair. But I am thinking that a proposal to give the garment workers a living wage and tie the whole market trend to The City That Knows How—well, the obvious choice for star ambassador would be you. If I set up a video conference with the C-Suite, I will need you to make the case that they should give their workers more than twice what anyone else is paying and convince them it is the smart thing to do and that they're going to get rich doing it."

Gretchen shrugged. "Okay, give me a few days."

"Not just that. Their keynote speech will be delivered by this hack from the government. But I am going to pitch them to put you onstage immediately after him, to make the case for domestic manufacturing and employing tens of thousands of people who have been out of work and, in many cases, out of their homes for years. The trade official will be the keynote speaker, but I want him to, in effect, be the opening act for you. And I want yours to be the message that gets these shareholders jumping out of their chairs and cheering. And our ambassadors will be spread throughout the crowd, reinforcing every word you have said." Eric seemed taken up by the idea himself, staring into the distance just as Gretchen had been doing a few minutes earlier.

Gretchen could not resist the temptation to bring him back to earth.

"Um, Boss, I think you are at risk for becoming an incurably naïve optimist. Do you really think we can pull this off?"

He shrugged his shoulders. "I dunno. You got anything better to do?"

She pretended to look at her social calendar. "Well, I did schedule myself some time to watch the paint dry on my kitchen wall. But I suppose I could postpone it."

24

∽

CHAPTER 24

The phone rang before the sun came up. Gretchen snatched it up and answered, too startled out of her sleep to react more calmly.

"Are you awake? Turn on the Channel Six news," Eric said.

She fumbled for her remote on the nightstand next to her bed. "What's happening?"

"Just get the news on."

As the screen lit up, the text across the lower third blared out in bold print, "1 Dead in Vigilante Attack."

Gretchen suddenly felt nauseous. "Did it involve one of mine?" she asked Eric.

"Just turn on the sound."

"Police said the man was a known gang member. A phone call at three fifteen this morning alerted them to an alcove off the street near Taylor and Eddie streets, where they found the victim's body. The officers found a knife still clutched in the victim's hand. He had suffered a fatal head injury, apparently from blunt force," reported the newscaster.

"Police said it did not appear to be a robbery, as the victim still had his wallet and cash. The location in the Tenderloin is just two blocks away from recent attacks connected to the city's new cleanup program."

Gretchen sobbed into the phone. "Oh my God, Eric, I hope we didn't cause this."

"Baby Girl," he replied, "you begged people not to get violent. Don't blame yourself for this."

Thinking back to those attacks after the payroll dispensation at the transit plaza, she suddenly sat straight up on the edge of her bed. "Eric, I have to make a call. I may be late to work this morning."

Before making her call, she went to the bathroom to splash cold water on her face. She returned to her bedroom and pressed a name on her contacts list to speed-dial the number.

"Mark, if you are responsible for this attack, I will give your name to the police, the FBI, and Interpol," she shouted into the phone when he answered.

The voice on the other end of the phone line did not sound fully awake. "What the hell are you talking about?"

"Don't play dumb with me. One of your thugs killed somebody on the streets last night. I want to know what kind of mob you are running, and why you are starting a gang war in San Francisco."

From the sounds on the phone, she could imagine Mark trying to rub the sleep out of his eyes so he could bring them into focus. "Gretchen, I don't have any thugs. I have a few dozen former police officers who work for me to provide undercover security at the racetrack and for company events. They do not kill people. They play strictly by the rules."

"Oh yeah? Were they playing by the rules when they beat up those men who tried to rob my workers on their pay day last week? Two of them had to go to the hospital."

He sounded exasperated. "That was different. Those men were threatening the lives of innocent people. And when my guys confronted them, they attacked, so my guys had to defend themselves."

"Well, how do you know one of your guys wasn't defending himself again when he bashed somebody's head in and left him dead on the street at three o'clock this morning?"

Mark's tone of voice turned angry. "My guys were not out on patrol last night. They only came in at my request to keep an eye on your payroll situation." Mark dialed down the anger in his voice to change the subject.

"Can we get together for dinner this evening to discuss the next phase of the campaign? I have got some ideas on how—"

"No, I do not want to get together. I am not sure if it is good for me to be seen in public with a mobster who employs an army that beats up people on the street."

"Babe, I told you that was not one of my people. And now that the campaign is picking up speed, we need to plan strategy to move to the next phase before the momentum fades."

She put steel into her voice. "When we made this agreement, you told me I had to work a minimum of five hours a week. I have already put in twenty-five hours, and it is only Wednesday. I have got other things I need to do today. Goodbye."

With that, she clicked the key to end the call. At moments like these, she missed having a desk phone that she could slam down on the hook to hang up on somebody who had pissed her off.

* * *

Seventeen-year-old Gretchen stood off to the side of the podium that had been set up in the high school gym. Several tables showed displays of science fair projects that had been submitted by students at the freshman, sophomore, junior, and senior class levels. Gretchen had won the award for the junior class. She and the winners at the other class levels were automatically entered into competition for the all-school award, the top science honor.

The sophomore and freshman winners had already received ribbons for third place and an honorable mention, respectively. Now just Gretchen and Bryan Taylor, the senior, were left. Mr. Griffin, the science teacher, adjusted the microphone on the podium before addressing the assembled students of all four class levels, who were seated on rows of brown metal folding chairs. As was aways the case, friends and social cliques clumped together in blocks of seats. In most cases, they were segregated by gender. And almost no freshman sat with juniors or seniors, though some had made inroads with sophomores and were seated on the periphery of some of the older students' groups. The rowdiest of the senior boys mostly gathered in pockets near the back of the gym.

"And now for the second place and first-place winners. Bryan Taylor designed and built a working model of a wind turbine that generates electricity," Mr. Griffin said. "Though his model is of course small in size —only large enough to turn on a light bulb or to charge a cell phone— his concept could be used on a much larger scale to provide energy for homes or commercial uses. Obviously, with our natural resources dwindling and, in light of the terrible effects that fossil fuels have had on the world's environment, we need more forward-thinking ideas like this to create sustainable energy. Excellent work, Bryan."

Students seated toward the front rows applauded wildly, while some of the boys sitting in the back hooted congratulations mixed with insults. "Way to go, nerd," hollered one. Bryan smiled broadly and briefly nodded his head, waving one hand above his head to acknowledge the applause. His face turned a bright red. Gretchen knew that Bryan was a confident and even sometimes animated boy when he was gathered with other science and math students but suffered extreme shyness among non-science people. Whatever burst of pride he might be feeling at this moment— probably the peak of his life experiences up to this point, she guessed— he must also feel terrified at having to stand in front of almost a thousand schoolmates. Earlier, before they had been called up front to stand in front of the crowd, Gretchen had glimpsed him several times checking to make sure his zipper was pulled up and securely fastened, and lightly licking the palms of his hands to use the moisture to smooth down the hair on the sides of his head. He had chronic cowlicks on the hair adjacent to each of his ears, and the smoothing had no lasting effect. But she nodded and smiled to boost his confidence. She knew that if she told him his cowlicks were still protruding, he might melt when it came his turn to accept his award.

Mr. Griffin cleared his throat to cut the students' chatter.

"Gretchen Vandella also built a working model. Hers demonstrates how microorganisms feed upon bacteria on objects' surfaces and in the soil, and how insects in turn feed on these microorganisms. The insects facilitate the fertilization and growth of vegetation, which provides sustenance for animal life. The animals consume the vegetation, and some of the larger wildlife also feeds on the smaller animals. Animals of all sizes digest their food and secrete excrement into the soil, which starts the cycle again by providing food for microorganisms. And the human race depends entirely on this ecosystem, consuming both vegetation and wildlife to live and thrive."

A number of girls in the middle of the student body clapped their hands and shouted, "Yay, Gretchen."

Mr. Griffin paused. "Thus, our two top science projects this year make detailed examinations of the serious ecological concerns facing all of humanity. One demonstrates one potential solution in the quest for renewable, clean energy production. The other illustrates the global impact that all species have on sustaining life itself. Our judges had a very difficult time choosing the best project between these two, which were submitted by some of the brightest students this school has ever seen. Indeed, they were even tempted to change the rules and award two equal prizes for our winners. But in the end, a choice had to be made."

The science teacher turned toward the two students standing to his side.

"Bryan, our world's quest to develop sources for sustainable clean energy has grown to become one of our top priorities. Your science project illustrated how one readily available source—wind—can help move the world forward while protecting it from further ravages caused by reliance on fossil fuels. We see your work as vital to science and to the world, and we hope you will continue to devote your considerably astute scientific mind to developing a broad range of sustainable energy sources. We see a bright future for you—no pun intended." A few of the people in the front rows chuckled. "Bryan, I am proud to present you the Second Place Award for this year's science fair."

Bryan's face reddened even more, and many of his friends in the front rows applauded loudly as he stepped forward to accept a plaque and a handshake.

Then, as the significance of Bryan's second-place achievement sank in, the cluster of girls seated in the middle of the assembly began shrieking congratulations for Gretchen. Startled at their shouting her name, Gretchen's face went from bewilderment to the sudden realization that yes, her project had won first place. She gasped and then pressed the palms of her hands over her gaping mouth. As Bryan returned to her side proudly carrying his plaque, she hugged him and tried to tell him how happy she was for him. But by this time, the noise from the students in the gym had grown too loud for her to make herself heard.

"And of course," Mr. Griffin said loudly into the microphone to quell the noise from the students, "that means that our First Place Award goes to Gretchen Vandella." Now the girls in the mid-section renewed their applause and shouts of, "Way to go, Gretchen."

Gretchen stepped forward to receive a handshake and her plaque. Accepting it from the teacher, she held it with her left hand against her chest facing forward. Mr. Griffin took hold of her right hand and raised it up above their shoulders in a sign of victory.

But now a new chant began to grow in volume and drown out the congratulations. It started with several boys in the cluster in the rows at the back of the gym and swelled as more boys in other sectors joined in.

"Lift your sweater and show us your tits. Lift your sweater and show us your tits," the boys shouted.

Mr. Griffin's face registered shock. Clearly unaccustomed to having to maintain discipline among uncouth boys, he sputtered, "Stop that. This is very rude." But he could not see who was chanting the phrase at Gretchen, and he did not leave his place at the podium.

The chant continued and grew in volume. "Lift your sweater and show us your tits. Lift your sweater and show us your tits."

After waving his arms ineffectually for more than half a minute, Mr. Griffin gave up and almost shouted into the microphone, "This assembly is dismissed. Return to your fourth period classes immediately."

A few dozen girls rushed from their mid-section seats to gather protectively around Gretchen. Those closest to her took turns giving her hugs and verbal reassurances, while those closer to the crowd turned and glared at the boys in the back.

Following Mr. Griffin's dismissal, students began working their way out of the rows of chairs and down the aisles toward the double-wide doors at the front. The boys from the back rows wore blank expressions as they blended into the crowd. Mr. Griffin was unable to identify any of those who had disrupted the proceedings.

Gretchen walked to her book locker in one of the hallways and deposited the plaque inside it. When she went to her fourth period class and sat at her desk, she stared forward silently throughout the class, neither volunteering to answer any questions that the teacher posed to the class nor chatting with other students sitting nearby. During the breaks before the fifth and sixth period classes, she spoke to no one but merely deposited and retrieved books from her locker. She remained silent during both classes, as she had in the fourth period.

After the final bell of the day, Gretchen took two textbooks needed for homework from her locker and slipped them into her knapsack, and slid the plaque between them so it would not get scratched. She walked home alone, unlocked the door, and walked inside. She set the plaque face-up on the kitchen table so her mother would see it when she got home from her shift at the restaurant after midnight.

Gretchen went into the bathroom to wash her hands. She lathered them with soap, rubbed them together, and rinsed thoroughly, but they still didn't feel clean. Then she lathered up a terrycloth washrag, scrubbed long and hard, and rinsed thoroughly again. Finally, in frustration, she almost tore her clothes off and turned on the hot water tap in the shower to warm up the water. Stepping in, she took a rough loofah and scraped first her hands, then arms, shoulders, legs, and every other region of her body that she could reach. The scraping left red marks on some of the more tender areas. Seeing the marks brought tears to her eyes, and Gretchen stood under the shower's stream of water with her head bowed, weeping uncontrollably.

25

The shareholders politely stood up from their luncheon tables to applaud. The official from the federal commerce department waved to the crowd, and then shook hands with the chairman of the clothing manufacturer's board. The chairman introduced him to a few other executives sitting at the head table, and then they all took their seats. Their lunch plates had already been removed before the speech, but now waiters descended on all the tables with silver coffee pots and began filling the cups of the two hundred people in attendance.

The chairman stepped up to the podium. "Thank you, Mr. Secretary, for those outstanding and encouraging words. We at Silk Industries feel so blessed that the founders of this company pledged more than fifty years ago that they would keep all production at our own factories here in the United States. We have had to compete with cheap foreign labor all these decades, but we think it was worth it. The quality of our products stands head and shoulders above the rest, and we can proudly put 'Made in America' on all of our clothing tags."

More polite applause followed.

"And now," the chairman continued, "we have a surprise speaker who was just added to the agenda in the past day or so. I am sure that you have heard the news about all the excitement up north in San Francisco. There has been a huge surge in civic pride as people are cleaning up the city and taking back the streets. Really, I haven't seen anything like this since I was a boy growing up after World War Two. It is truly phenomenal."

He paused for a moment glance over to the door from the kitchen. "So, it gives me great pleasure to introduce the woman who started it all. You may have read the profile in the *Gazette* a few days ago about Gretchen Vandella. She was downtown San Francisco one day and looked around herself, and she saw that the streets were dirty with grime and trash, and she also saw homeless people living on those same streets. People too poor to get into housing, even too poor to feed themselves. There were dots there staring us all in the face, but only she actually connected the dots. In hindsight, it seems pretty obvious, but none of us saw it. It took this brilliant young woman to connect the dots, to put together a program, to pull together the resources to support it, and to connect with both the government and the private sector to make it happen.

"She is cleaning up the streets. She is giving honest jobs to the homeless. She is restoring civic pride to the point that normal citizens are out defending the homeless against those who would attack them. And she was so audacious as to give her organization the title, The City That Knows How. And friends, I think she has proven her point. I give you Gretchen Vandella."

With that, he signaled his aide to open the kitchen door, and Gretchen marched out. Knowing that her client produced some of the most elegant clothing in the country, she had chosen not to try to impress the audience with fashion. She wore a smart business suit in her signature cranberry red, closed at the neck, sensible heels. There was a conservative scarf visible above the neckline, bright but not so colorful as to make her look less than serious.

She did not stop at the head table to shake hands with dignitaries but approached the podium directly. Standing behind it and looking out at the crowd, she angled the microphone downward to point toward her mouth. She had typed out a speech back at the office, and then reduced it down to bullet points that she could easily commit to memory. She wanted to speak directly to this crowd without fumbling over notes or staring at a teleprompter. Using a mnemonic trick she had learned from a popular actress, she had further reduced the bullet points to the first four letters of her name: G, R, E, and T.

"Good afternoon. I think most of you are old enough to remember when it was popular to say, 'Greed is good.' Now, I don't agree with that when greed is the overriding passion, the only thing that drives you. But a little bit of greed is what motivates us to do better. We all want better things for ourselves and our families. A little bit of greed pushes us to take advantage of opportunities. It pushes us to look for strategies that will create more opportunities for us to accumulate more wealth."

Gretchen held her hand in a saluting position over her brows to screen her eyes from the glare of the spotlights. "Tell me. I was told this is a shareholders' meeting. Raise your hand if you own shares in this company." Almost every person in the room raised a hand.

"Now raise your hand if you bought shares in order to make money." Again, all hands went up.

"Now raise your hand if you only bought shares because the chairman here seems like a nice guy, and you think he needs your help."

No hands.

"Okay, I am glad we got that established." Turning to look at the chairman at the head table, Gretchen said. "In all fairness, sir, you probably really are a nice guy. But nobody here cares." Laughter broke out in the audience. This woman was different. No one had dared taunt the chairman in any past meetings.

"So, I gather that most of you have heard about what we are doing in San Francisco. We are cleaning up the streets. We are putting the homeless to work at good, honest jobs with a living wage so they can afford to get housing and stop living on our sidewalks. We are restoring civic pride to the point that ordinary people are willing to get involved again.

"Now, some anonymous donors have put huge amounts of money into the pot to make all this happen. Raise your hand if you think they are giving away millions of dollars just because they are nice guys who want to help out."

No hands.

"Now raise your hands if you think the letter G had something to do with it. Yes, 'good' starts with G, but so does 'greed'."

Every hand went up.

"Okay, now let's move on to the letter R, which stands for reality. Here in Los Angeles, you have enough room to spread out, so nobody gets too close to anybody else unless you are in love or at war," she said, eliciting a few laughs. "Yes, here people do not usually get into your personal space unless they are either going to kiss you or hit you. If I have heard correctly, I believe you all have a three-foot radius around each of you. That is your personal space, and it is almost universally respected.

"But in San Francisco, we have only forty-nine square miles of space into which we cram an average of eighteen thousand people per square mile. The very rich and the very poor live almost side-by-side. We have twenty-million-dollar mansions, but less than a mile away tenants are struggling to pay the rent for a studio apartment with four or five people crammed onto a few mattresses on the floor. And those people are not buying clothes from this company, Silk Industries. If they buy anything, it is from the second-hand thrift stores. We have got presidents and CEOs whose limousine drivers have to run interference against street beggars when they open the doors for the executives to get out of the car."

Gretchen paused to let her audience picture their chauffeurs fending off panhandlers.

"It did not take much for the wealthy class to figure out that it was in their own interest to improve the lot of the poor. If nothing else, it would make their own lives more comfortable. In other words, some Good might satisfy their Greed. If nothing else, it might make life a bit more comfortable for the very wealthy."

The audience had fallen silent, so Gretchen took the microphone out of its holder and stepped around in front of the podium so the audience could see her completely. "Are you all following me? Can you see that life for the rich might get easier if the poor were not right up close in their face?"

A murmuring of assent greeted her. She paused for a moment while a number of people turned to their neighbors and exchanged stories from their own experiences of being accosted for handouts.

"So, we are recruiting homeless off the streets to clean up those streets. Some of them have administrative skills, and we are putting them to work to manage the program. Some have skills in construction, others in maintenance. We are putting them all to work. Because we recognized the letter R, reality. If those people do not start working, then we will never solve the problem."

At this moment, the crowd stirred as someone at one of the tables made a bit of noise. Candy stood up from her chair at the table in question and raised her hand. "But I have heard that there have always been poor people in San Francisco. How do you think having a few of them pick up trash is going to change things?"

Right on cue! During the planning session at Aurora before this trip, Gretchen had asked for a volunteer to raise this objection. Even Eric raised his eyebrows questioningly when she selected Candy. So many of the other ambassadors had long experience in working these meetings and seminars and knew how to handle comments and conversations that inevitably ensued. Most members of their crew saw Candy as the bimbo of the group and did not give her any credence. But Gretchen had struggled against those same assumptions and resentments in her own career, and it took years to gain respect for her intellectual skills even though she had a graduate business degree from a respected university. She wanted to develop Candy into a proper ambassador. This small break would give her a taste of bigger things to come.

Several shareholders tried to hush Candy and motioned impatiently for her to sit down. "No, she raised a good point," Gretchen interjected. "In fact, that brings up another point. The letter E. Expectations. What do we realistically expect is going to happen as a result of all this? Are we going to end poverty? Are we going to end hunger? Are we going to create universal brotherly love and peace?"

Gretchen held her hand out toward Candy.

"Of course not," Candy barked, "and I think it is phony of you to expect us to believe that." The people around her gasped at her harsh words and again motioned impatiently for Candy to sit down, but Gretchen called out, "Our expectations are not to solve all the world's problems, but to at least address what we can while still addressing a bit of our own greed.

"You are absolutely right that it would be phony. Tell me, what is your name?"

"Candace. My name is Candace Reynolds."

Gretchen extended her hands out toward Candy in a sign of respect. "Well, Ms. Reynolds, it takes courage to call BS when you see it, so thank you for calling it here. But you bring up an important issue. We cannot create such high expectations. If we do, then no matter what we accomplish, it will be a disappointment. No, we are not eliminating homelessness or poverty. We are only trying to clean up the streets. But while doing so, we are creating opportunities for some people to lift themselves up by the bootstraps."

Now was the time for the T in her bullet points of GRET. But Gretchen would not let on to the audience what the T stood for.

"And more importantly for the people in this room. I hear that you are going to create a new line of clothing for consumers who cannot afford your more elegant lines. Well, how about if you create a brand identity that will attract those customers? Now, hear me out. You already manufacture clothing domestically, here in the United States. You are one of the only companies in the world that does so. What if you build new garment factories in every region of the country, and start hiring the homeless or the underhoused to work in your factories? Pay them a living wage, just like we are paying our street cleanup workers in San Francisco. We pay our workers double the national minimum wage. Yes, you heard that right. Twice as much as the minimum wage. If you create an army of new workers who are getting a second chance in life, they will owe it all to you. And when those workers are buying new clothes, who do you think they're going to buy them from? *This* company! And when the rest of the poor people in the country hear what's going on, who do you think they're going to buy their clothes from? *This* company! And when the United States government tells the whole country that it needs to start manufacturing clothes and other products domestically again and pay its workers a living wage, who is it going to hold up as a shining example? *This* company!"

Gretchen had been gradually raising her voice with each exclamation of "*This* company." By now she was almost shouting into the microphone. She raised the fist of her free hand in the air as she held the microphone at arm's length in front of her and shouted.

"And who is going to get enormous profits from this movement? Who is going to gain the biggest market share you could ever imagine?"

Candace was the first to jump to her feet. "*This* company!"

Nick stood up from his seat at the other end of the room. "*This* company!" he shouted.

Now several of the real shareholders stood up as well, shouting, "*This* company!" Eventually, someone started waving his arms like an orchestra conductor to get them all to shout it in unison, and they started chanting "*This* company!" Gretchen stood holding her arms up and out to the sides for several moments while the chanting continued, and then she turned at last and approached the head table. She bowed slightly at the waist and reached out to shake the commerce secretary's hand, and then the company chairman and other corporate officers. With the other ambassadors continuing to lead the chant, "*This* company," Gretchen waved at the crowd, turned, and walked through the kitchen door.

26

❧

CHAPTER 26

Her cell phone rang, and Gretchen glanced at it on her desk. The caller i.d. said it was Mark Fischer calling again. She had ignored the previous six calls, but the man was obviously not going to take the hint and quit. She picked up the phone.

"What."

"Can we please talk?"

"What do you want to talk about?"

"Us, eventually, but first I wanted to tell you that my sources in the police department think the killing was done by a rival gang. There's a lot of drug trafficking in that part of the Tenderloin, and something of a turf war is brewing," Mark said.

Gretchen did not sound like she believed a word of it. "So, what, you got one of your buddies on the police force to plant a story that would get you off the hook?"

Mark grunted into the phone in what might have been a laugh if the mood had been lighter. "Hey, make up your mind. One minute you are saying that I am running an organized crime mob that murders its opponents, and the next minute you say I am so close to the police that they would tell lies to cover up for me. It is one or the other, babe. It can't be both."

She was about to make a snarky response but caught herself. That was true. If the police really did suspect another gang, they would not have confided in Mark if they thought that he ran a criminal organization. On the other hand, she had only his word for it that anyone in the police department had said any such thing. She would call her own contacts at the SFPD later for confirmation. Since starting her cleanup program, she had gotten to know several insiders on the force.

"So, you are saying your gang didn't do the killing, it was somebody else's gang?"

"I do not run a gang."

"Okay, if you say so."

He put a note of impatience into his voice. "I told you that the security people I work with are all retired police officers. The gang members who got injured before had attacked them with weapons, so they defended themselves forcefully. But they are not killers. If you can't trust me on something so basic as knowing right from wrong on matters of life and death, then I don't know how we can continue this partnership. If you think that a mobster is funding your work, you won't have the confidence to do your best. And if I have to worry every minute whether you are going to report me to authorities every time you don't understand a decision, then I can't very well continue this arrangement either."

"What are you saying" she asked.

"Gretchen, it is up to you. Don't make up your mind tonight while you are angry. In fact, don't decide tomorrow or the next day either. But by Friday, I expect a decision from you. Either you are in for one hundred percent, and you trust me too, or else you are out. There is a severance clause in your contract, so you will get two months' pay if we quit this relationship. But it is up to you. Make up your God damned mind."

Apparently, Mark had called from a desk phone, because Gretchen heard him slam it down angrily.

27

CHAPTER 27

The morning did not start auspiciously. Forty-five minutes into their work shift, the power went out at the Aurora office. All the computer screens suddenly went dark, and of course most of the ambassadors had not saved any of their work before the computers crashed. When the power eventually came back on, everyone would have to recreate whatever documents they were working on when the lights went out.

And to make matters worse, a client had contacted Eric and canceled an upcoming branding project due to an unexpected business crisis in that company's finances, which in turn could create a financial crisis for Aurora. A cloud of gloom seemed to hover above the office.

Gretchen's phone rang, and she answered. "Can you step into my office?" Eric asked.

"Sure." She wondered why he had not just stepped outside his office door and waved her in, as usual. Why the phone call?

She closed the door behind her without being told to do so and took a seat. Eric's face looked gloomy.

"Silk Industries' chairman just called. His people had been calling around to their contacts in San Francisco, and there seemed to be some confusion about whether you are still affiliated with The City That Knows How. After that talk you gave a few days ago at their meeting in Los Angeles, everybody was fired up to move forward. Now they're not

"

so sure, because they're not sure if you are still part of it. Do you know what's causing the confusion?"

Gretchen sat in silence for a moment. Her recent good fortune had seemingly sprung out of nowhere in a flash. Could it really disappear as quickly in a flash too?

"I don't know," she said, slowly shaking her head. "I had an argument with Mark Fischer the other night. And he said that if we could not resolve the matter, he would end our working relationship. But I thought he was giving me several more days to think about it."

She outlined the cause of the conflict, hoping Eric would understand. The criminals who were attacking her program's workers were themselves being attacked, and Gretchen suspected it might be Mark's security forces. She suspected they might actually be a criminal gang.

She looked into Eric's eyes to see if he agreed.

"You suspect them of criminal activity. Tell me, do you have any direct evidence that Mark Fischer or his people are involved in any criminal doings? Did they attempt to steal anything from your workers?"

"Um, no. I am just reading between the lines here."

"I see,' he said. "But before we start guessing what's between the lines, let's look at the lines themselves. What facts do we have?"

"Some people tried to rob some of my street workers right after they got paid."

"And was it Mark's people who tried to rob them?"

"No. Mark's people stopped them and beat them severely when the robbers tried to attack them."

"I see. So, Mark's people were protecting your workers from criminals. Let's move on. Somebody killed a member of the same gang that tried to rob your workers. Do we know who killed this criminal?"

"No. The police think it might have been a rival gang in a turf war over drug trafficking."

"I see. And do you have any evidence or reason to suspect that Mark is involved in drug trafficking?"

"Well," she stammered, "no, but I don't think he is telling me everything."

"Stop," Eric said, holding his palm toward her. "We are only examining facts right now, not what you think might or might not turn out to be a fact. So, you have no evidence that Mark is involved in selling illegal drugs. Do you have any evidence that his security people constitute a street gang?"

"No. Mark says they are all former police officers."

"I see. And now I will ask for a few facts not directly related, but I think they may play into it. Am I correct in believing that a romantic relationship was developing between you and Mark before these questions came up regarding his security people?"

She pressed her lips together and looked down at his desk. She nodded her head up and down in small, quick jerks. "Yes," she whispered.

"I see. And did I understand you correctly to say earlier that Mark said, if you don't trust him on such a basic issue as murder, he could not continue either the working relationship or the personal relationship?"

A tear started to escape from the corner of her eye, but she dabbed at it with the edge of her knuckle before it could smear the makeup on her cheek. Eric pulled a tissue from the dispenser on his desk and handed it to her. He gave her a minute to compose herself.

"So, let's summarize what we have so far. And set side what impact any of this might have on Aurora's business with Silk Industries. Let's focus just on The City That Knows How and, to a lesser extent, you personally. Feel free to jump in and correct me if I got any of this wrong. First, based on absolutely no evidence, you suspect that Mark Fischer is running a ruthless street gang that is involved in drug trafficking and murder. Second, based on absolutely no evidence, you have basically told Mark to his face that you think he is lying when he tells you that your suspicions are wrong. Third, based on items one and two, you are willing to throw away your leadership of an organization that is already benefitting many thousands of homeless people, merchants, and residents of this city. In other words, based on absolutely no evidence, you are willing to destroy all the work that you and so many others have put into this noble project."

Her eyes no longer produced any tears. But she sat still, staring blankly.

"And, just let me add a personal observation here. These past several weeks, you have been happier than I have seen you in all the years that you have worked here, and that includes the times you singlehandedly pulled off marketing coups that looked like magic. These past few weeks, you have had a genuine smile on your face instead of the phony frozen grin you put on for our clients. You have spoken to people with enthusiasm in your voice, not the controlled pitches you use for our branding projects. I don't want to be so crass as to suggest that it is just because you are finally getting laid, but you have had a real glow on your face, and not just because of a new line of makeup. You have been truly happy."

Eric sat up straight behind his desk.

"But, going back to items one and two on our list, based on absolutely no evidence, you are willing to throw away your happiness and go back to being the Ice Queen. And in case you have kept your eyes and ears closed all these past several years, that is what your younger colleagues call you. The Ice Queen, because you were always so cold and seemingly heartless that they were amazed you had gone into marketing. Those who know your personal history rebuke them and tell them to show respect. But the truth remains that you were so cold that no one dared to connect with you on a personal level. You were alone in the world. And based on absolutely no evidence, you are going to throw away your happiness and become alone in the world once again."

Gretchen still said nothing, nor did she move.

"Look, why don't you take the rest of the day off and go home. If you stay at work this afternoon, I think you will cause the temperature in the entire office to drop at least twenty degrees. And after all that's happened today, I don't know if I will be able to afford the heating bill to bring the temperature back up to normal."

Gretchen rose from her chair, went to her cubicle, turned off her computer, picked up her handbag, and left the office.

28

❧

CHAPTER 28

The cell phone jarred her awake in the dark. "Is this Gretchen Van-della?" asked a voice she did not recognize. She fumbled for the light on her nightstand. The clock read three thirty.

"This is Gretchen."

"Ms. Vandella, my name is Laurie Rizzo, and I am a nurse at the Stanford Hospital. Our emergency room is treating a patient who was brought in unconscious, and we found your name and number on a sheet of paper in his pocket. Do you know a man named Mark Fischer? That's Fischer with a C after the S."

Gretchen gasped. "Oh my God. What's happened to Mark? Is he going to be okay? Can I come see him?"

The nurse's voice remained calm. "Ms. Vandella, are you his next of kin?"

"Next of kin? Oh my God, is Mark dying? What do you mean, next of kin?"

"Ms. Vandella, the staff searched his wallet and pockets, and they found your name and number in several areas of his effects but nobody else's contact information. Yours was the only one. The doctors are giving emergency treatment right now. But if any complications develop that require permission to proceed, they would need permission from the next of kin."

138

Without thinking, Gretchen blurted out, "Yes, I am. I am his wife. Is he at the hospital on the Stanford campus? I can be there in forty-five minutes."

She brushed her teeth and dressed within five minutes, and quickly drove over the hill to the freeway. It took her just twenty minutes to drive the thirty miles to Stanford because the freeway was empty at this time of night. The highway patrol usually turned a benevolent eye toward speeding on this stretch of highway, so she pushed the speedometer to ninety miles an hour most of the way down the Peninsula. She cruised onto the huge campus, popularly known as The Farm, because it was built on Leland Stanford's farm while he served in the U.S. Senate back in the 1800s. Formerly situated amidst rural surroundings, its hometown of Palo Alto grew with the rest of the San Francisco Bay Area region to become an essential part of a major metropolitan area.

Gretchen found parking near the hospital entrance and almost ran to the door. Fortunately, no line of people caused any delay at the reception desk at this early hour of the day. She signed a form falsely claiming to be Mark Fischer's wife, and the receptionist gave her directions to the waiting room nearby.

"Will I be able to see him?" Gretchen asked.

"When the doctors have finished their work with him, they will let you know," the receptionist answered.

The waiting room had a few magazines but otherwise offered no distractions. Gretchen pulled out her phone, scanned her emails, looked at text messages on the encrypted apps but could not bring herself to reply with erotic teases to the lonely old men or the thousands of others who followed her. She checked the other applications but found no communications that interested her at all. She opened one of the magazines and leafed through one page at a time, barely seeing the contents and registering no information from any of them. The wall clock made an audible click as the second hand hit each of its sixty stopping points while it circled the face. At some point Gretchen noticed that her foot was tapping against the floor, and she thought it was working out to ten foot taps per every three seconds. With nothing else to occupy her mind, she started doing the math in her head to determine how long it would take her to tap her foot a thousand times. She happened to glance up at the ceiling and saw that each ceiling tile had a lot of small dots in a pattern that repeated every three rows. Again doing the equations in her head, even as her foot continued tapping, she calculated that each tile had two hundred and nineteen dots. The ceiling had a length of twenty tiles and a width of twelve and a half. She would need to check to find out the number of dots in one of the half tiles, but it looked like the total would probably come to—

"Ms. Vandella? Are you Gretchen Vandella?"

"Yes, that's me," she answered. The woman at the door wore a doctor's scrubs and still had gloves on her hands. She had pulled her mask down from her mouth to dangle in front of her throat, and she used the backs of her fingers to push her glasses up to the top of her head.

"How is Mark? Is he going to be okay? What happened to him, anyway?"

"Mr. Fischer is in stable condition, considering what he has gone through tonight. He has regained consciousness and is resting peacefully. Apparently, he was stopped in traffic and got rear-ended by someone suspected of driving under the influence. The other driver walked away from it uninjured, though I think the police arrested him. But your husband got banged up pretty badly. The concussion was not severe, but we want to keep him here several days for observation. More importantly, the impact dislocated a vertebra in his upper spine, so he will have to wear a neck and back brace for some time to come. It is absolutely essential that you keep your husband from engaging in any physical activity that could result in permanent injury."

Gretchen almost spoke up in objection when the doctor said husband, but then she remembered that she had claimed to be Mark's wife so that she would be admitted to see him. "Thank you, doctor. When will I be able to see him?"

"We have just transferred him to a private room. Please follow me."

They walked together down a series of hallways. When the doctor stopped and turned through a doorway, she called out, "Mr. Fischer, your wife is here waiting to see you."

"My wife?" Mark was propped up on several pillows. Gretchen saw that he could not turn his head toward the doctor, that a large brace was completely immobilizing his upper body and that metal guards on either side of his head prevented him from turning. She rushed forward and clutched the guard rail on the side of bed, and moved her face directly in front of his so that he could see her without straining.

"Baby, my poor baby," she said, tears springing from her eyes. "The doctor says you are going to be all right, but I have to take good care of you."

The doctor stirred behind her. "I will leave you two alone. Ms. Vandella, here is my card. Please call me tonight for an update, so I can fill you in on his condition and the types of care that you will need to give him when you take him home."

Gretchen slipped the card into her pocket. When the doctor left, she turned to Mark and said in a low voice, "I had to tell them that I am your wife in order to get in here. They were asking for your next of kin, so it sounded serious. I don't even know if you have any family, or if they are even in California."

Mark attempted to smile. "My wife. My, how quickly things can change."

Gretchen leaned across the guard rail and kissed him tenderly on the lips. "Baby, I am so sorry for doubting you. Of course, I trust you and I trust your security people. Can you forgive me?" She held his hand, and she felt his thumb rub against the back of her wrist.

"You were right to have doubts," his voice rasped. "You don't accept things at face value, which is one of the reasons I selected you for the non-profit. And it looks," he added, turning his eyes downward toward the brace on his neck, "like it is going to be doubly important for you to keep a wary eye on everything. While I am laid up, you are going to be running the whole show. I am sorry that all the responsibility is landing on your shoulders so suddenly, but you will be able to handle it."

Gretchen said nothing, just gazing into Mark's eyes. Finally, she stirred. "When they release you from the hospital here, you can come stay at my place. I will take time off from work to care for you."

"Nonsense," he said. "Thousands of people are counting on you to run The City That Knows How. And Eric needs you at Aurora. I can have skilled nursing at my own home, medical professionals who know exactly how to give me the care that I will need. We both need you to take care of business."

Gretchen squeezed his hands lightly and kissed him again. "We will discuss that more later. Meanwhile, I should let you get some rest. I need to get home to get ready for the day. I think I need to go kick some asses."

29

"Wow, so this is the office for your city cleanup project, eh? It is not big, but it is all yours."

Gretchen had invited Candy to come downstairs to her office for lunch, which had just been delivered to the office door. "I hope you don't mind a Chinese vegetarian meal in a takeout container," Gretchen said. "I have never done any entertaining here, so I don't have dishes or utensils."

"No problem." Candy pulled the wooden chopsticks out of their paper sleeve, broke them apart, and lifted a slice of eggplant out of her lunch container. "So, I hear this side gig of yours has gotten really busy lately."

"Yeah, that's part of the reason I asked you down here. I have gotten so busy that I have had to let some of my regular routines go. I was wondering if you had any interest in picking up a small side gig yourself?"

Candy looked surprised. "Me? I always thought you hated me."

"No, I don't hate you. If I acted harshly or cold, it is because I have gone through the same things as you and I am trying to help you avoid some of the mistakes I made on the way up. I get frustrated when I see someone in danger of repeating some of my mistakes. If I sounded mean, I was not angry at you, I was angry at myself when I learned a hard lesson doing the same thing you were doing at that moment. I learned a lesson but forget that you have not necessarily learned it yet."

Gretchen finished chewing some bok choy and swallowed. "Look, both of us have gotten where we are because of our looks. Of course, we have brains, but our brains alone would not have opened the doors that you and I have been able to walk through in our careers.

"And you are the sexiest ambassador of the entire agency, so I can guess that you have probably never been given any credit for your intelligence. People see your face, your blond hair and your boobs and your shapely bubble butt, and they instantly think they know everything about you. And let's be honest, I put those things in the wrong order. They see your boobs, then then the blond hair. If they even look you in the face, I bet they don't make eye contact."

The frank talk about body parts seemed to break any tension that might have been hanging in the air between them.

"Tell me about it," Candy laughed. "I could be giving my doctoral dissertation and the professors would be trying to figure out if I was wearing any panties under my skirt. Not," she interjected suddenly, holding up her index finger, "that I am in a PhD program at present, although I might go for that if I can save up enough for the tuition. But sometimes I think I could be speaking in Swahili for all the attention that anybody pays to what I say."

The two shared a knowing smile and raised their hands above their heads to tap each other's palms together in a high-five.

Gretchen nodded. "Okay, you already know what you have got. I was being totally serious when I said you are the sexiest looking ambassador at Aurora. You know it, I know it, and all our coworkers know it. If some of them don't seem close to you, it's because they recognize that you have a natural advantage over them, so they are trying to compete as best they can. But put all that aside. That's not what I wanted to talk to you about."

Now Gretchen zeroed in on her eye contact with Candy.

"Look, I need to ask first if I can trust you to keep details confidential. If we do this, I will be sharing some things with you that I don't want to get out. Not that there are dark personal secrets about my hidden life as an international spy. It is just that I would be revealing some things that took me years to compile, so I do not want them shared with other people who would get to use the information for free."

"But you are giving me free access to it?" Candy asked.

"Yeah, well, maybe you will make use of it, maybe you won't. But like I said, I would like to help you so you don't have to go through all the trials and errors that I did."

Gretchen told her what the hourly wage would be, starting at five hours a week. "Wow, yes I am interested," Candy exclaimed. "What would you want me to do?"

Gretchen pulled out her personal iPad. "You are familiar with Countenance, the social media app where people mostly post their own pictures? There is also a Chat function on it, and you can keep in touch with people who follow you."

"Yeah, I have got a few dozen people I chat with on Countenance."

Gretchen opened the app to her profile page. "Here is my business page. You notice the top pictures are professionally done, and they feature great hair, great makeup, elegant clothes, and sexy poses."

"These look like they could have been taken at some of our shoots for Aurora."

"Some of them probably were." Pointing on the screen, Gretchen added, "Check out the number of followers."

Candy gasped. "Oh my God, you have got more than a hundred thousand followers. How do you handle that many?"

Gretchen pulled her chair around to the side so she and Candy could look at the screen together while the iPad lay flat on the corner of the desk. "I upgraded my Countenance subscription so I could create distribution lists on the Chat function. Here is the general list, which goes to all one hundred thousand." She tapped on the list, and a chat field opened. She typed in, "Good afternoon. I hope you have eaten." Then she clicked the arrow on the right to send the message.

Candy put her elbows on the desk and leaned in to watch as dozens of new messages loaded into her chat feed. "Those are people just saying hi back to you. How do you get time to read all these responses?"

"I don't. Like you said, most are just saying hi. Maybe one or two out of every ten is giving specific details about what they ate for lunch. Maybe one of every fifteen or so are telling me not only the entire menu of the meal they just ate, but also what ingredients they used and how they prepared it. I don't actually read all those messages. But they think I do, and that has helped me build my personal brand."

Candy's eyes glanced back at the distribution lists. "What's this one labeled LOM?"

Gretchen tapped her young colleague's arm. "Ah yes. You and I are experts in brand management. LOM stands for 'lonely old men'. You notice the list has more than four thousand? I don't actually know all their ages. Some might only be in their twenties, so they are not really old. And many of them are probably not really lonely, but they have certain characteristics and have made certain types of responses that have led me to lump them into the same demographic, the same distribution list. It is almost like the algorithms that direct millions of social media users to specific types of targeted advertising, except that I have assembled this and other lists manually, by myself. There is a list labeled MOS for 'my older sister', and another is MYS for 'my younger sister'. Women who treat me like a sibling, either asking for advice or giving me advice whether I ask for it or not. There is FF for 'fashionable females' and FM for the guys. I can market brands for personal clients to specific groups, for a fee, of course. But let's look at the LOM, lonely old men. That list gets slightly different treatment."

She tapped the LOM list and the chat field opened. "Okay, are you going to do this with me? Can you handle this task for me about one hour a day, five days a week? There will be a few other items you would have to do, but daily contact with my followers takes top priority. If you have time, you might share personal messages from me or even yourself once in a while with some of the most active people on the lists, especially the lonely old men. You will get to know which ones are the most active within a few days. But are you in?"

"Absolutely."

"Then let's introduce you to the LOM." Gretchen tapped the camera icon on the chat field, held the iPad up and moved her chair next to Candy's. She put her arm around the younger ambassador's shoulder and leaned her head against Candy's. Both immediately smiled into the camera, and Gretchen clicked the icon to take the picture. Scrutinizing the image, she nodded her approval and typed the caption, "Here I am with my girlfriend Candy. I told her about you, and she is impressed." Gretchen raised her eyebrows to ask if the message needed amending, but Candy gave a thumbs up. Gretchen clicked the arrow to send.

Gretchen got up and moved her chair back to its usual spot behind the desk. She picked up her chopsticks and scooped a bit of the remaining rice into her mouth. She nodded toward the iPad still on the desk, which was lighting up repeatedly with new messages. "Looks like you have become famous. Dozens of these men will be just saying hi to me, but even more will be trying to get information about you and figure out what I meant when I called you my girlfriend. Some will assume it is innocent. But a huge number will wonder if we are bisexual, and if we are lovers. I don't have to tell you that this is a huge male fantasy, to be in bed with two women together and all three of them going at each other equally. Do not—repeat, do not—ever confirm or deny that we are lovers. If you need to give any reply at all, make it something innocuous like, 'Oh, Gretchen and I work well together. She knows how to make me sit up and take notice, and I know how to get her attention too.' If they ask what kind of work we do together, or whatever else they think it might be, maybe once every few weeks we will treat them to a photo of the two of us together in bikinis. We certainly do plenty of shots like that for the agency."

"How does Eric feel about this?"

"He supports it. My personal brand here supports what the agency does. We all win."

Candy leaned forward. "When do I start?"

"You just did. Later, I will give you information how to log onto the account from your own device, and how to access the gallery of pictures. Give the general list a picture or short video clip of me two or three times a week and give the LOM one every second or third day. Say something only slightly provocative to the LOM. They will fill in the details from whatever their own fantasies might be. Include some of your own pictures if you like, and it is okay if you tease them sexually just a bit. But keep it classy. It will hurt both of our personal brands if they think we are being cheap. Any questions? If not, let's get back to work upstairs. Eric said he has a big client coming on board soon, so we should do our research."

"Gretchen," Candy said as she stood up from her chair, "I can't tell you how much this means to me. I had no idea you were running your own private brand, and now you are letting me help. I have felt so alone at this agency, but now I feel like I have a friend."

"You have got lots of friends in the agency. You play a vital role in this team. Each of us has a different role, and we all think you have done a fabulous job playing yours. But I want you to expand so you can take on other roles too. And you are about to get a lot more friends here," Gretchen said, nodding toward the iPad in her hand.

30

CHAPTER 30

Gretchen looked out at the half-dozen reporters. Two were from TV stations, and their camera operators had placed their tripods front and center. A woman from the East Bay represented several suburban papers. Another came from Marin County north of the Golden Gate, one from the Peninsula, two wire services, and one from the daily *Journal* in the city.

She had consulted with Eric on the best backdrop for this announcement. They first considered setting up at the Palace of Fine Arts. With its Greco-Roman architecture and beautiful lagoon in the foreground, it would make for gorgeous pictures to accompany the story. But then Candy, who had come into Eric's office on an unrelated matter, stated the obvious. This announcement was coming from The City That Knows How. It absolutely had to be given with the Golden Gate Bridge in the background. Eric and Gretchen looked at each other and mockingly slapped themselves on their foreheads with the palms of their hands as if to say, "Of course, why didn't I think of that?"

As was her practice, Gretchen did not use a podium because she did not want to obstruct the cameras' view of her from head to toe and all points in between. And she used a clip-on microphone with a feed that each of the reporters could plug their own recorders into so that it would not be necessary to obstruct the view of her face with several microphones.

"This is an exciting day for us here in the city, and I think it is exciting news for other areas of the state too," she said. "Today I have here with me the chairman of Silk Industries, which is best known for producing some of the most elegant attire for women and men in the country. Silk is launching a new line of clothing more suited to the popular market. Together, we are opening a garment factory for the new line here in San Francisco. Yes, that's right. We are bringing manufacturing back to the city. And my organization, The City That Knows How, will provide laborers who will earn a living wage. Just like the people who are cleaning up our beautiful city, these garment workers will earn double the national minimum wage, with benefits."

Unlike past events, Gretchen did not attempt to plant ambassadors in the group to seize the floor with softball questions. These reporters here today all knew each other and would quickly recognize an attempt to steamroll over them. So, she had prepared herself for hard questions. The first came from the reporter for the *Journal*.

"Ms. Vandella, this sounds very noble and all, but how on earth is this company's clothing going to compete with that of more established companies using cheaper overseas labor?"

"I will let Mr. Michaels answer in more detail," Gretchen replied quickly. "But essentially, because the materials are produced domestically and the manufacturing is done locally, Silk will realize tremendous savings on shipping and distribution, and it will avoid the problems with the overseas supply chain that all American industries suffered in recent years. And because we are using American materials, and manufacturing in American factories, and putting Americans to work, we think the American public will support us when they go to their local shopping malls.

"And by the way, I am wearing a sample of the clothing that will be coming out of Silk's new line," Gretchen said, sweeping her hands to indicate the pants, blouse and light jacket she wore this day. "As you can see, the material is good, the fashion is contemporary, and the prices will remain affordable. This particular outfit was part of a limited test run that

Silk did with its current manufacturing facilities, which are also located here in the United States. Silk is an American company, employing American workers to produce American goods for American consumers."

One of the TV reporters asked before anyone else could say a word, "The Bay Area is the most expensive real estate in the country. Won't your competitors just set up facilities in a low-cost region and also claim to be domestically produced?"

"We would welcome the competition," she said. "Will they also pay double the federal minimum wage? Will they also use domestically produced textiles? And will they also keep their profits here in America, or will they send their money to overseas accounts to avoid paying American taxes? I think Silk Industries can answer yes to every one of those questions except for the last one. Silk keeps its profits here in America and it pays its fair share of taxes. I would challenge Silk's competitors to do the same. And now, let me introduce Mr. Robert Michaels, who can answer your questions about Silk Industries."

Michaels stepped forward and accepted the clip-on mic from Gretchen. Rather than attach it to his lapel, he held it in front of his mouth and spoke directly into it, probably far too loudly for the recorders that the feed was going to. "I want to say I just met this young woman two months ago, and I have been overwhelmed by her energy, her shrewd mind, and her outstanding leadership abilities. When she made this proposal to our board, we asked all the same questions you are asking right now. And we made a business decision that it was the right thing to do, and we expect it to be highly profitable. Now, I would be happy to answer any questions."

As Michaels began fielding questions, Gretchen's mind wandered. She began examining the area where they stood. They had chosen a spot near the edge of the bay, with the bridge dominating the background. A large cargo ship had just sailed under the bridge and was gliding past.

A familiar bus pulled up near where the press conference was still going on. The door opened and, as she watched, the entire crew of Aurora's ambassadors disembarked. Tears suddenly sprang to Gretchen's eyes when she realized that every one of them, the men included, was wearing an outfit from Silk's new line of clothes for the mass market. Without interrupting Michaels, they circled around to join Gretchen where she stood in the rear, with the bay and bridge behind her. Candy led the way and stood next to Gretchen as the others all lined up in an arc to the left and right. Gretchen noticed that the two TV camera operators were panning across the line of ambassadors, dwelling especially on the women.

Michaels was all but forgotten by now. As he finished a long-winded response to a question, one of the reporters called out, "Who are these people behind you?"

Michaels turned and looked bewildered. Gretchen stepped forward and took the microphone from him, and clipped it on her jacket. "I mentioned before that the outfit I am wearing is an advance sample of the type of clothing that Silk will include in its new line. But this line is not a one-trick pony. Each of these people is modeling a sample of the many fashions the company will be producing."

Gretchen swept her arm across the length of the arc, and the ambassadors one by one stepped forward to make a quick turn to show his or her outfit. Though the ambassadors were much more than models, they each had professional training as models and knew how to strut their stuff both for a live audience and for cameras.

Later, after the reporters had left, Gretchen approached Heidi and asked how they happened to show up in Silk fashions. It had been a godsend that gave a much-needed added dimension to the otherwise pedestrian press conference.

"Believe it or not, Candy did it. She went to Eric about a week ago and said we had to do something to support you. He called Silk's vice president for operations and told him to get us thirty outfits pronto. They came through."

"Candy?" Gretchen asked. "Amazing."

31

CHAPTER 31

The name on the caller i.d. prompted her to answer on the first ring. "Mark, how are you? Did the physical therapist work with you today?"

The voice on the other end of the line sounded cheerful for a man who had been restricted to home for six weeks. "Hey, babe, I saw you on TV tonight."

She wanted to hear about that. "Did they show all the Aurora ambassadors? Did they play any part of my remarks? Did they play anything about Silk Industries?"

Mark chuckled into the phone line. "Babe, Channel Eight did four full minutes on your story. They covered the street cleanup again, the agreement with Silk Industries, and they spoke to national economists on the impact this could have locally and, if it spreads, regionally or even nationally."

"Oh my God," she said slowly. "Did you record it? Oh, please tell me you recorded it."

"I recorded it. I also recorded Channel Six. You should set your digital video recorder to tape all the major newscasts for the next several days."

"I will, but you still didn't answer my question. Did you work with your physical therapist today?"

"Yes, yes, I will probably be able to leave the house and do some business in a few days, provided I have someone else do the driving and I use a couple of crutches to keep the pressure off my spine."

"Do you want me to drive for you?"

"Absolutely not. You have far more important things to do.

"Did the doctor say if you can spend the night at my place? Or me at yours?"

"That might not be a good idea. I would have to break the law," he said.

"What law would you break?"

"The lady always comes first."

She snickered. "You just lie on your back and see what I can do. And I will, at least once. Twice is better."

* * *

Eighteen-year-old Gretchen sat with a cluster of girls in the first three rows of seats set up for the senior class in the school gymnasium. While the other students walked through the doors onto the basketball court and looked for friends with whom to sit, the girls chattered about their classes, and colleges and universities their parents had taken them to visit and the results of their various applications to the institutions. One of the girls excitedly told them that her parents had bought her a car. She still had only a learner's permit and so could only drive with a licensed driver accompanying her in the passenger seat, but she was progressing rapidly and hoped to get her license soon. If she gained admission to a far-off university, she would ask her parents to pay the extra fee for her to get a campus parking permit so she could keep the car near her room in the dormitory. Gretchen avoided saying anything; her own mother could certainly not afford to buy her a car, and the cost of living in a dormitory would absolutely stretch beyond her means. Gretchen hoped to win a scholarship to pay part of her college costs, but she also expected that she would have to hold down a part-time job to help cover rent in a roommate arrangement. Depending on the location, she might need an apartment with multiple roommates to keep the rent affordable.

As Gretchen and her friends continued talking, they heard a commotion at one of the doors that caused several of the girls to roll their eyes. Some of the rowdy boys had come into the gym laughing gruffly and bellowing at each other's jokes. As usual, they crowded into the back rows of seats. Mr. Beck, the vice principal, kept a visible presence near the back of the gymnasium, so the boys kept their remarks clean and refrained from shouting insults at students in other parts of the hall, as was their usual practice. Even so, their very presence cast a pall over the atmosphere for the cluster of girls around Gretchen, and the conversation turned to memories of times the boys had disgusted or, in some cases, humiliated the girls.

When the more than three hundred and twenty students of the senior class who were present that day had taken their seats, Mrs. Gallagher, the principal, stepped up to the podium at the front and adjusted the microphone. The statuesque woman wore her platinum hair in an elaborate wave. The girls had often gossiped about how much money the principal probably had to spend on hairspray alone to keep that high hairdo in place. As was the fashion a few decades earlier, she wore light pads under the material on her shoulders to give her upper torso a more angular appearance. She always wore dresses or skirts; the students could not recall having ever seen her in a pants suit. Though her stomach appeared flat—whether through diet and exercise or by a tight corset—Mrs. Gallagher had a large bosom that seemed to defy gravity as it jutted forward above her abdomen. The girls had often speculated that the woman must wear an extremely uncomfortable wire-supported brassiere, of the type that many wags called an "over the shoulder boulder holder." Her face was attractive and may well been quite pretty in her younger years.

"Senior class of Parker High School, please come to order," Mrs. Gallagher said into the microphone. She enunciated her words clearly and crisply, speaking at a pace slow enough so that no one would miss a word but rapid enough to keep things moving along. "You still have a bit more than two months before graduation, but we have some important business to take care of. Before the school yearbook can be printed, we need to take pictures of the lucky individuals that you students and the faculty together have selected for certain honors."

She paused to look out at the students and permitted herself a smile. "So, I hope you dressed well today. The winners of these honors will come to the podium after I call out your names, and then you will have your photograph taken at this space to my left." Mrs. Gallagher extended her hand to her left to indicate an area where a photographer had set up two lights and a white background screen.

"The first honor is for the student voted Most Likely to Open a Business. Now, I know that many of you are already selling merchandise on the Internet, and some teachers mentioned in the Faculty Lounge that at least one of you is already running an online dating service. But when we conducted the elections for these titles last week, we told you to choose someone who you think would open a physical brick-and-mortar business with a real street address, not just a website or post office box."

She held up a piece of paper and read from it. "Most Likely to Open a Business. Mr. Larry Baker, please come forward."

Larry Baker got up from his chair, located about halfway between the front and back, several seats in from the aisle so that his neighbors had to stand to let him get by. Polite applause accompanied him as he walked toward the front and shook hands with the principal. She handed him a small plaque and directed him to the photo area, where he held the plaque against his chest and posed for a picture.

"Larry, before you return to your seat, what kind of business would you like to open?" Mrs. Gallagher asked into the microphone.

Larry walked to the podium and faced her. She took to microphone out of its holder on the podium and pointed it at him. "Originally, I wanted to open an independent bookstore," he said. "But now, with so many people abandoning physical books, I think I would have to also specialize in electronic reading machines. I would probably also want to carry tablets and possibly some popular brands of laptop computers. But my primary focus would still be books."

"You have an excellent vision of the current and future market," the principal said. "No matter what medium comes to dominate the field to accommodate authors' new books—whether it is print, electronic, audio, or video—we will always need works by classical as well as new authors to hold society together as it moves forward." Larry nodded his head in a slight bow and then returned to his seat.

The assembly continued with more awards for various titles. As might have been expected, Most Likely to Be a Movie Star was won by one of the cheerleaders, a blonde with piercing blue eyes and a bright white smile. Most Likely to Graduate from an Ivy League University went to Bill Nichols, who had assisted Bryan Taylor on his project when Bryan won second place to Gretchen in the Science Fair the previous year. In a tribute to non-academic students who worked better with their hands, there were honors for Most Likely to Build a House, Most Likely to Build an Engine, Most Likely to Be a Sculptor, and others.

The schedule called for the senior class assembly to last for two hours, and the clock was showing it had almost ten minutes left. Most of the students relished the change in routine, the opportunity to skip their fourth and fifth period classes. But others had grown impatient and were fidgeting in their seats. The school routine in middle and high school had conditioned them for almost six years now to sit in one place for an hour at a time. Anything more than that tended to make them a bit antsy.

Mrs. Gallagher stepped up to the podium again.

"And now we have just one more award to announce. This is for the class valedictorian. I will warn you ahead of time that we gave more weight to the faculty's vote on this one, though the votes were similar from students. Both the Parker High faculty and the senior class expressed pretty much the same conclusions, so I do not think you will be disappointed." She extended her hands toward the students in a gesture of inclusion.

"Each and every one of you has some outstanding talent that you can use to make this world and your lives in it better. Some of you know how to make the environment around us beautiful, some of you have the skills to make it practical and easier for the rest of us. Some of you make music, and some of you make beautiful stories as you weave words and ideas together. Some of you have great mathematical skills, and some are adept at the sciences. I could go on but the list might never end. You all are very valuable to society.

"The person whom we have together selected as your class valedictorian represents all of you and all of your outstanding qualities. This person has a perfect four point oh grade point average and has demonstrated great skills in all of the academic, artistic, and physical coordination areas of education."

She raised her arms out to her sides. "Please join me in congratulating your class valedictorian," here she paused dramatically, "Ms. Gretchen Vandella."

Gretchen sat stunned in her chair. The girls around her squealed with delight, and soon began chanting, "Gret-Chen, Gret-Chen, Gret-Chen." She still did not move, staring wide-eyed toward the students in front of her, who had turned to cheer her. Finally, the girls on either side of her grabbed her by the elbows and propelled her to her feet. "Go on, get up there, Silly," said one of them. Gretchen crab-walked sideways to make her way through the thin spaces between the girls' knees and the seats in front of them, until she reached the aisle where she could walk unhindered to the front of the gymnasium. When she arrived at the podium, she reached to shake hands with Mrs. Gallagher as the previous award winners had done. Uncharacteristically, the normally undemonstrative principal grasped Gretchen's hand and raised it up high in a sign of victory. While the students continued to applaud, the girls in Gretchen's cluster raised their voices louder in their chant, "Gret-Chen, Gret-Chen, Gret-Chen."

Facing the crowd, Gretchen suddenly felt a sickening sense of dread in her stomach and déjà vu in her mind. She recalled the Science Fair award presentation in this same place the previous year, and she feared the uncouth boys in the back row would ruin her day again. The boys had shattered her moment of personal triumph on that occasion by calling for her to lift her sweater and show them her breasts. And that had sickened her, calling to mind the attack outside the school dance in her sophomore year.

But this time was different. Mr. Beck prowled up and down the aisle on the left side of the seats, while the girls' gym teacher, Miss Granger, eyed the boys hungrily from the aisle on the right side as if she would almost welcome a fight. Gretchen smiled inwardly at the sight, remembering Miss Granger defending her with a baseball bat when four boys assaulted her. Today, it almost looked like the teacher was anxious for any excuse to grab one of more boys by their ears and drag them bodily outside. The boys refrained from shouting any rude, crude, or lewd comments. They probably feared Mr. Beck, but some had probably learned to fear Miss Granger even more.

After the photographer took a portrait of Gretchen holding her plaque, the students were dismissed to go to their sixth period classes. Her circle of girlfriends surrounded Gretchen as they made their way out of the gym, excitedly congratulating her and making suggestions on what topics she should touch on in her valedictorian speech at the graduation ceremony.

"World peace, of course. Everybody talks about it, so they'll expect you to say something about it," said Carla.

"Solving homelessness," suggested Sally. "That might be easier to achieve than world peace."

"How about racial justice?" asked Carolyn, whose complexion was a dark olive due to her mixed heritage.

Terryanne, whose dry humor often snookered listeners who were unaware that a gag was being played on them, held up a forefinger and said in a serious tone, "These are all important concerns, I am sure, but here is one that is not receiving the attention it is due from the press, and certainly not our elected leaders. 'Tis a question that has stumped the wisest of minds among us, and the less wise as well. To wit: is it legally and morally proper to serve pineapple on pizza?"

Sixth period passed like a breeze. Gretchen had already thoroughly read the history chapter that was under discussion in class, and listened with one ear as the teacher discussed it and asked questions of other students. Fortunately, she kept her cell phone on silent vibration only, because she received text messages with congratulations and more suggestions for her speech almost every two minutes. Text messages had long since replaced the paper notes that students pass to each other during class.

32

∾

CHAPTER 32

Eric caught Gretchen's eye and nodded discreetly across the office toward the stairs down to the photo studio. She nodded slightly. He apparently wanted a discussion away from the others' eyes and ears, so it would not do to make it obvious that they were leaving at the same time to talk. She sorted some items on her desk, picked up a file of old photographs, and drifted toward the door. She went downstairs to what had originally been the front of the old theater but was now the agency's photography studio.

Several minutes later, she heard the door open above and behind her, and Eric came down the stairs. He signaled her to move to a corner of the studio less visible from the office door. She wondered what was behind this need for secrecy. Eric obviously had something big to tell her. Well, she did too, but she had not made her decision yet on the possible paths facing her. Would she bother telling him? That would depend on what he was meeting her in the studio to tell her.

"What's up, Boss? Lovely weather we are having, don't you think? Hey, how about them Giants?"

"Smart ass." He grinned as he glanced one more time over his shoulder to make sure no one else from the office had followed them. His grin continued as he turned to talk in a confidential tone. "I got a call from Silk Industries. They've been invited to speak in Washington,

D.C., at a congressional committee hearing. The topic is bringing manu-facturing back to the United States, but Robert Michaels got a heads-up from the committee chairwoman that they are also going to be talking about paying workers a living wage. He said this is a direct result of our involvement. Obviously, I think he was not referring just to the Aurora Marketing Agency, but also to The City That Knows How."

Gretchen reached out and held both of Eric's hands. "That is wonder-ful. I am very happy for Mr. Michaels. When do they want him to testify?"

"Next month," he replied. "He called to ask the agency for support, both on research for his testimony and also laying the groundwork with committee members. He wants us to assemble a team of a dozen or so ambassadors to go to Washington in a few weeks to make courtesy calls at the offices of the various Congress members on the committee."

Gretchen nodded. "That makes sense. Our ambassadors can lay the groundwork. Give background material to the aides, do some glad-handing with the congress members, maybe even wear some of the new Silk clothing. That way, by the time Mr. Michaels appears before the committee, members will already be well on their way to liking what he says."

"Exactly." Eric turned and faced Gretchen squarely. "That is why I asked you down here, away from the others. The team we send to Washington is going to need a strong leader with drive, intelligence, and outstanding organizational skills. I won't be able to go, because I will have a number of things here that I need to attend to. I know you would be a tremendous presence there as the head of The City That Knows How. I wanted to know if you could go in a dual role. Would you be willing to lead the group as the newly appointed vice president of the Aurora Marketing Agency?"

Gretchen put one hand to her chest and willed herself to take slow, steady breaths. She could feel her heart suddenly thumping against her ribcage. She waited for it to calm down a bit before answering. "You are offering me the job of vice president of this agency?"

"Yes," he said with a wide grin. "We are getting a huge number of potential clients calling to inquire about our services and we are going to have to expand soon. I can't do this alone. You have proven that you have what it takes to take on the shared management of the agency."

Seeing hesitation in her eyes, he quickly added, "Oh, don't worry about your side gig. I would absolutely want you to continue running The City That Knows How. But you might need to hire staff so you could delegate more of the work there. That's what we presidents do. We hire smart people and then delegate the work to them. We very seldom do any of the work ourselves." Eric offered her a pad of paper. "You should write that down for future reference."

"The ambassadors and I are well aware of that, Boss. No offense, but it often comes up in conversation that you don't do any of the real work around here," Gretchen laughed.

"Vice president." She stared vacantly toward the old movie screen, which was now used as a "green screen" for videos. The camera crew could take a video of an ambassador and later, in editing, project a different backdrop onto the green screen to make it appear the ambassador was filmed on location outdoors or in an office, or even in another country. It allowed the agency to create an illusion.

"So, what do you say, Baby Girl?"

Gretchen looked at Eric and put on her diplomatic smile, which she ordinarily reserved for work events in which she did not necessarily care for the client's brand identity. "It sounds wonderful. But there is one issue that might make it difficult, if not impossible. That will be for you to decide, and I will be okay with whatever decision you make."

She paused for a moment, unsure how best to tell him.

"I am pregnant."

33

CHAPTER 33

"You are pregnant? That's wonderful. We have to make plans."

Mark started to raise his wine glass for a toast but halted midway. "I don't know if you will be drinking during the pregnancy. I think I read that moderate amounts of alcohol should not cause any harm to the baby, but of course it is entirely up to the mother to decide whether to imbibe."

Gretchen lifted her glass, which Mark had filled without asking, and clinked it against his before taking a small sip. She had called immediately after her meeting with Eric and insisted that they meet for dinner at a quiet restaurant near his home. He could drive short distances now, but she did not want him traveling far. The conversation would take precedence over the menu.

Mark continued speaking even though Gretchen had said nothing more yet. "We should probably get married soon, before you begin to show and can't fit into whatever gown you select for the wedding. For the ceremony, we could rent out one of the largest wineries in Napa, if you like. Or, if you prefer a church wedding, we could book Grace Cathedral in the city. It all depends on how many guests you want to invite. The cathedral can seat a thousand people, but you might need more than that now that you are becoming so famous. I can keep my side of the guest list relatively small, though there are some people I would be obligated to invite out of professional courtesy. And if we are at the cathedral, we can book a banquet room at the Fairmont Hotel for the reception dinner afterward, so the guests only have to stroll across Huntington Park without driving to get there. I have friends in senior management at the Fairmont who will make sure everything goes perfectly. And as long as we are there, we can book the penthouse suite for our wedding night. Have you ever seen the view from there? Oh, it is magnificent. You are just going to love it. What do you think?"

Gretchen's face betrayed no emotion. "You seem to have worked out everything yourself. You don't even need me."

His eyes dazzled as he continued. "If you like, we can honeymoon in Paris, which is absolutely wonderful this time of year. Or, if you are feeling more adventurous, we could try Shanghai. The sights on The Bund in Shanghai are fantastic. In fact, if you like, we could stretch it into a tour of Southeast Asia, with stops in Korea, Japan, Vietnam, and Hong Kong. Have you been to Thailand? Oh, you will love Thailand. And maybe we could finish up with a few days in Singapore before flying home."

Mark stopped and looked at Gretchen. "Babe, you haven't said anything. What do you think? Do you want Europe or Asia? Or, now that I think of it, we might as well do both. We can start in Paris and hop down to Rome before flying to Shanghai. You will need to take a full month off of work, but I am sure Eric won't mind because you will be taking a maternity leave anyway. Oh, you are going to love it. What do you think?"

Gretchen took another sip of wine, this one deeper than the first. She leveled her gaze at Mark's eyes. "It sounds very much like all of these plans of yours involve a wedding."

"Yes, of course, darling. If Grace Cathedral or a Napa winery would not work, there are other—"

"Was I supposed to be part of this wedding?"

Now Mark looked impatient. "Don't be silly, of course you are the star of the event. Everything will center around you; I can't even select the color of my cummerbund until you have—"

"You seem to have everything worked out already, except for one thing. Were you planning to ask me if I want to marry you?"

Now Mark's face froze, his mouth hanging open as if he were about to speak. He did not move or speak for a full ten seconds. "Well, I assumed—"

"What gives you the right to assume anything, let alone something so important as how I am going to spend the rest of my life? When I came here tonight, I was full of love, and I probably would have said yes on the spot if you had asked me properly. But now I am not so sure."

Mark's voice took on a pleading tone. "Babe, I am so sorry. I just got so excited when you told me the news. I didn't stop to think."

"Exactly. You didn't stop to think. You just decided that whatever Mark Fischer wants, that's what Mark Fischer and whoever he drags along with him are going to do no matter what anyone else thinks. Is that how it would be if we were married? You decide you want to go to Shanghai, so you just call down the hallway, 'Drop whatever you are working on, dear, and pack a bag, because we have to catch a flight'? Or if you decide that I shouldn't have a career anymore, you are just going to call Eric and tell him I quit? All you have to do is say, 'Oh, I didn't stop to think,' and everything will be forgiven?"

She finished her glass of wine and threw her napkin onto the table. Mark tried to put his hands over hers, but she snatched them away. "Please, we can talk about what you want over dinner."

"Nope." Gretchen stood up from the table and retrieved her purse, which had been hanging by its shoulder strap over the back of her chair. "Enjoy your own fucking dinner. I will pick up a cheeseburger on the way home, and I will eat alone so I can give some thought to whether I was to spend my life with somebody who thinks he can make all my fucking decisions for me without asking me. I am leaving. I have got a long drive."

With that, she turned on her heel and walked out of the restaurant.

* * *

Eighteen-year-old Gretchen pulled the cheerleaders into a conspiratorial circle. She whispered her plans to the girls and asked if she could count on them.

"Absolutely," Karen said as the others nodded in agreement. "All of us thought it was terrible what happened, and we will be glad to help set it right."

Gretchen thanked each of them by name and touched each of their arms or shoulders before moving across the central quad of the school to speak to another group at one of the outdoor lunch tables. So far, she had agreements from the sports teams, the cheerleaders, and the female members of the school's scholastic club. The plan was rapidly coming together.

34

CHAPTER 34

"Ms. Vandella, do you have the audacity to come here and lecture the esteemed members of this august body on how to end homelessness?"

Gretchen looked at the congressman and tried not to judge him by the stereotypes that immediately leapt into her mind. Seated behind the dais adjacent to his colleagues, the man appeared to have made the common fashion mistake of dressing for the age and shape he was in during the period of his fondest memories rather than the current reality. As a result, his white dress shirt strained against its buttons. The shoulders on his suit jacket were stretched too tight. Gretchen did not want to think of what might be beneath, but an unbidden image arose in her mind of his T-shirt being too small, stretched tight across his torso and not long enough to cover the lower part of his belly. She had met many such men in her career, some of them clients, and a large number of them lived in their past glory days, not the present, and they still wore the same clothes they owned back then. Aside from reflecting that attitude on the way they dressed, they also thought the solutions that worked in their younger years should still work now, decades later. An unfortunately large number of them also recalled that women were not allowed to be leaders during those long-past years, and the same should hold true now.

"Congressman., I am not telling you how to legislate your program at all. I was asked by your colleague to come tell you what has worked for our specific program in San Francisco."

"Well, young lady, not every place in the country is like San Francisco," he said, cutting her off before she could continue. "In fact, I don't think anyplace else in the country is like San Francisco. You have got a lot of strange people out there."

Gretchen forced a smile onto her face, because that would prevent her from blurting out a snarky retort. "Congressman, we realize that. But if we can make something work in San Francisco, the most expensive place we know of, then there is a chance that our ideas can be adapted to the conditions in other areas of the country. You and your colleagues here have a much broader view of the country than I, and in your wisdom, you may be able to pick bits and pieces of our program and adapt them for a more comprehensive campaign for the rest of the country."

The congressman glared at her for a moment longer, and then spoke into his microphone. "Madame Chairwoman, I yield back my time."

"The representative from Missouri has yielded back his time. The chair recognizes the gentlewoman from Massachusetts."

The Massachusetts representative looked at least twenty years younger and more than a hundred pounds lighter than her colleague from Missouri. She also smiled in a much more encouraging manner.

"Thank you, Madame Chairwoman. Ms. Vandella, the information we have here says that your cleanup and assorted other programs have put just two thousand people to work. The last report that I saw indicated that San Francisco had more than five thousand homeless people living on the streets."

Gretchen had gotten this question so many times that she could respond immediately.

"Yes, Congresswoman. We never expected to end homelessness completely with our program. But the people we have given jobs to are getting places to live, paid for out of their own earnings. And some of them are inviting their homeless friends to come stay with them. Some of the stores and restaurants are experiencing increased business as a result of the cleanup, and they are hiring more people to staff the increased demand. And the increase in economic activity is spurring entrepreneurs to start up new businesses, and they are hiring too. This program illustrates the power of building the economy from the bottom up instead of the top-down approach that is usually attempted."

"Ms. Vandella," the congresswoman continued, "we just heard testimony from Robert Michaels that, based on your success, he has opened a garment factory in your city and is giving workers good pay and benefits. Do you really think his company has any chance to make a profit on this? It sounds like a recipe for disaster, paying high wages to homeless people in the most expensive city in the country to produce clothing for the poorest people in the country. What on earth did you put in his drink to make him go along with such a plan?"

Laughter rose from the galley behind Gretchen. The hearing had drawn a packed house of spectators.

"Congresswoman, the decision was made by the full board of directors at Silk Industries, and I assume they did it because they expect to reap huge profits for their shareholders. I am certain they did not vote unanimously on this venture just because they are nice guys. Yes," she added quickly, "I have met them, and they are indeed nice guys, and nice women too, but their first duty is to their shareholders. They would not do this unless they expected financial success. That goes both for building a factory in San Francisco, and also for staffing it with the formerly homeless and paying them a living wage, double the national minimum wage, in fact. We are The City That Knows How, so we are going to make this work."

35

CHAPTER 35

After receiving a disturbing phone call, Gretchen drove to the Civic Center Plaza across the street from City Hall. Finding a rare open parking space on the street, she fed the parking meter and walked into the center of the open space that faced the mayor's office on the second floor of City Hall across the street, above the ornate brass doors at the entrance of the domed building. Many political demonstrations occurred on this space in the plaza precisely because the shouts and other noise would aim directly at the windows of the mayor's office.

Gretchen walked directly between two groups of people facing off in hostile stances in the plaza. On one side were workers she recognized from the TCTKH clean-up program. They stood idle, unable to proceed with their work because the other group blocked their way. The group on the opposite side carried signs with slogans such as "Fair Pay for Fair Work" and "Stop Scabs." Gretchen moved quickly between the two groups. Many on both sides started point at her and calling out to their friends, having recognized her from pictures in the newspaper and on TV.

Spotting the supervisor for the clean-up workers, Gretchen approached. She was glad she had worn flat shoes instead of high heels, but her choice of footwear put her at a height disadvantage now. She had to tilt her head back to speak up to the man. "What's the situation here?"

"Gretchen, you might not remember me. My name is Bill Lincoln, and I supervise the Civic Center crew."

"I remember you, Bill. You were with me when we did the first clean-up in the financial district. So, what's happening?"

Bill nodded toward the opposing group. "Those are city workers. They say public works canceled plans to hire more workers because we are doing the work. They say we are taking away their jobs."

She nodded. "Okay, Bill. You just keep your crew together, and don't let these guys intimidate you. I don't think I will need your help. Let me try to talk to them on my own. You just keep your crew here and tell them to be prepared to resume work when I clear the way."

Gretchen walked across to where the city workers were marching in a long oval circle carrying their signs. A very large man, a giant both in height and girth, stepped out of the group and stood in front of her. She estimated his height at about six feet and seven inches, and surely, he topped the scales at more than two hundred and seventy-five pounds. The man towered over her as she drew to within three feet of him. She put her hands on her hips to support herself as she leaned back to look up at the man's face. "What is your name, sir?"

Unbeknownst to both of them a reporter and photographer had just exited City Hall. Seeing the crowd in the plaza, they approached quietly. The photographer ducked behind the reporter to pull her camera and a long-distance lens out of her bag without attracting attention.

"I am Jack Graves," replied the big man, "and I represent these workers in the union. You are that woman who's helping those scabs over there take our jobs away."

Gretchen took one hand off her hip and pointed her finger at the man.

"Well, Jack, you are right about one thing. My name is Gretchen Vandella, and I am the president of The City That Knows How." She turned and waved at her clean-up crew, and she raised her voice loudly enough for all to hear. "But you are wrong to call these people scabs, Jack. Scabs are non-union people hired to take away union members' jobs."

"Yeah, that's what they're doin'," he said, raising his voice as well.

Gretchen held her index finger up toward Jack's face. "First, my workers *do* have their own union. Every crew has a shop steward who can call me directly if anything is not going right. They earn good wages with benefits, and we stick to strictly agreed-upon rules to give them the best working conditions that we can."

Now she turned to face him square on. "But Jack, something else you said disturbed me even more. How many of your workers have been laid off?"

The man looked like he had been caught off-guard. "Who said anybody has been laid off? Why, have you heard something? Is the city planning a layoff because of your people?" Jack had now raised his voice almost to a shout. Most of the city workers had stopped marching and now stood watching the exchange.

"No," Gretchen replied loudly. "When we first set up this program, the head of public works assured me no city workers would lose their jobs. And you just now confirmed that nobody has been laid off." Now she raised her voice almost to a shout and started wagging her index finger in his face. "So, where the fuck do you get off telling your members that my crew is taking away their jobs? They haven't lost any jobs. If anything, their jobs have gotten easier thank to the people employed by The City That Knows How."

By now, all of the city workers had stopped marching in the oval with their signs, gathering instead around their union rep to his left and right, crowding to get close to Gretchen. Meanwhile, on Gretchen's side of the standoff, the cleanup crew also gathered behind her. They looked like they were ready to throw punches, to do physical battle to defend her, but Bill held them back. The boss, Gretchen, had told him she would try to handle it on her own, so he would not let them charge. But his crew stood ready to leap to her defense if things turned ugly.

Jack, the union rep, tried to rally. "The city told our union it would not budget any more positions next year because there ain't enough work to justify it. And there ain't enough work because your people are doing it."

Now Gretchen raised her arms above her shoulders and nearly shouted at the city workers. "Did you hear that? He admits that you have not lost a single job. He is only talking about budget negotiations for next year. You men are not losing a thing. But meanwhile, Jack here wants the city's streets to get dirty again so he can negotiate with the city for more money next year.

"But who gets blamed for the dirty streets if my people are put out of work? Does Jack get a single bit of criticism? No, but everybody will accuse *you* city workers of being lazy. Everybody will say *you* city workers are overpaid, though I know you barely get enough to support your families. Look, I know you all do fantastic work, and your union represents you well. My people do fantastic work too, and their union represents them well too. We are all working for the same goal, and my people are not taking anything away from you."

Jack stood still, unable to articulate a response. So, Gretchen pressed forward. "So, let's end this now. Go back to work, and let my people go back to work. We are all friends here. Don't let anyone tell you otherwise."

Gretchen turned toward Bill and his crew. "Give me one of your trash bags. We are going to get back to work." She took a bag and walked into the middle of the city workers, bending to pick up scraps of paper on the ground. Bill motioned the crew forward, and they all followed suit. After standing and watching for a moment, several of the city workers joined the cleanup crew and began picking up litter.

36

CHAPTER 36

The photograph on the front page caused a shit storm. Above the fold, spread across four columns, readers opened their morning newspaper to the image of David against Goliath. But this David did not even have a slingshot. The seemingly tiny woman in the picture pointed her finger into the face of a giant bear of a man. She had no weapon. She had no advantage in size or strength. She had nothing but defiance in what appeared to be the face of mortal danger. And by all appearances, the giant bear was losing the battle.

The picture's worth exceeded a thousand words. In just the morning that it appeared, local and regional political pundits easily racked up millions of words. Reporters trying to get comments were unable to reach political figures, who were waiting to see which way the wind would blow before making any statements. But by the noon hour, employees in scores of buildings throughout the city had posted the picture on office bulletin boards and on the walls of their company breakrooms. Lunchtime gossip quickly gravitated to the image, with debates ping-ponging between admiration for the hot babe in the picture and support for organized labor. Look at her, many would say—if I ever end up in a street fight, I hope she is on my side. Yeah, others would say, but unions brought us good wages, weekend days off, time and a half for overtime, and health benefits. Of course, came the response, but she is not opposing unions. Her people have a union too. And she's not afraid of anything. Just look at her.

At the Aurora Marketing Agency, Eric had taken the almost unprecedented action of diverting all calls from his desk phone to those of the ambassadors. The volume of calls had bogged down his schedule, and he needed to make some important contacts with important people. The ambassadors each had a sheet of talking points from which they could answer questions. As with all their assignments, they could improvise responses as long as they did not deviate too widely. But if any questions arose that ranged too far outside the agreed-upon scope of the mission, they would either dodge and pivot to another topic or, if the questioner persisted, politely decline to answer.

The morning was decidedly darker for Gretchen.

Downstairs in her own office, Gretchen gave thanks that she had installed an old-style answering machine that broadcast callers' messages in real time, so that she would not have to log in to listen to all of these tirades again. Sitting at her desk and writing responses to emails on her computer, she could listen to the many phone messages as they came in. It seemed that a small percentage of the messages consisted of congratulations from well-wishers who had seen the newspaper picture, left by people who had never met Gretchen and had not heard of the cleanup program before. But a much larger portion of the messages—the vast majority—frightened her because they sounded so threatening, anonymous callers blasting her for not supporting the city's union workers. She feared the blow-back would spill over to the Aurora Marketing Agency. She did not know whether Eric would let her remain with the agency after all this controversy.

She stood up and stretched her arms to the sides and then toward her back. She walked to the front window and looked out through the blinds at the traffic passing by on the street. She gazed without focusing, letting her mind wander. Several teenagers walked together on the sidewalk across the street. The group suddenly stopped and pointed at something out of her line of sight, and Gretchen watched to see what had caught their eye. The youngsters stooped and picked up armloads of paper from the sidewalk and carried the refuse to a nearby trash bin.

The phone rang yet again, and Gretchen heard her outgoing recorded message. "This is The City That Knows How. Please leave your name, number and message after the tone. Thank you." As she watched the teens across the street, she kept a modicum of attention on the phone.

"Gretchen, this is Mark. Listen, I wanted to let you know that—"

"Mark, it's me." When she heard his voice on the machine, she had raced across the room to pick up the phone before he had a chance to hang up. "How are you, baby?"

He sounded like he had just run a mile. "My phone has been nonstop. But more important than me, how are you holding up?"

She sighed deeply. "I am sorry if I made trouble for you. I don't dare talk to Eric upstairs. I heard the agency has been pretty much turned upside down since the *Journal* ran that photo this morning." Her voice broke into a sob, but she struggled to avoid crying. "I am afraid I created a lot of trouble for everybody."

"Gretchen— "

"Oh, Mark, I never wanted to start a fight. But that union rep was intimidating my people, and I got pissed off when I saw how he was distorting the facts to manipulate the city workers. If I had known a photographer was there, I never would have started a fight."

"Gretchen—"

"And now I have fucked up everything," she continued, openly wailing and letting the tears run down her cheeks. "I am sorry, Mark. If you want my resignation, I will write you a letter and email it to you as an attachment before the end of the day."

"Gretchen, would you shut your God-damned mouth for a minute!"

She caught herself at the harsh tone on his voice. "I am sorry, Mark. I didn't give you a chance to talk yet. I know you are pissed off and have a lot of things you want to say to me. I will shut up."

"Finally. Thank God." Mark paused to collect himself before speaking. "I was not calling to request your resignation. I am not here to bawl you out or criticize you. Are you sitting down and breathing calmly now?"

"Yes." She sniffed and reached for a tissue to blow her nose.

Mark continued. "Okay. I was calling to tell you I got a call from the governor's office. Although your name is on all the paperwork for the nonprofit organization, they apparently did some digging and figured out that I was connected somehow. The governor wants to know if we would help set up similar programs in other parts of the state. Babe, The City That Knows How is a hit. People love it. And they love you."

Neither of them spoke for several long moments.

"Are you listening?" Mark asked. "Did you hear what I said.?"

"Yes. You mean I am not in trouble?"

"No, babe, you are not in trouble. Quite the opposite. The state Chamber of Commerce wants to know if you would speak to its members at its next monthly meeting."

Gretchen sniffed and reached for another tissue to wipe her eyes. "They what?"

"They want you to talk about getting the economy moving from the bottom up instead of the top down. They like what they're seeing in San Francisco. They think it represents an approach that will work in other regions too."

Her voice still had a meek, mousy tone to it. "You say I am not in trouble?"

37

CHAPTER 37

The overflow at the party would probably cost Gretchen a major portion of her monthly operating budget, but she did not care. The extra food alone would set her back, and then there was the alcohol. She had stepped out to the parking lot to talk privately with a new contact, and she marveled at how many large bins had already been filled with empty bottles for every type of booze she had ever heard of, and for many she had not. Remembering back to how she and neighborhood friends made extra money when they were children, she wondered if stores still paid deposits for empty pop bottles, and if children still made the rounds pulling their little red wagons to collect them. Even if very few of these bottles in the bins were for pop drinks, Gretchen figured she and her friends could have attended many Saturday matinees from the money they would have made from this haul.

Tonight's event all started at a meeting with the crew leaders and shop stewards. Every two weeks, Gretchen met with them to hear of any complaints, and recurring obstacles in various parts of the city, and any common trends or themes that they were witnessing on the streets. The group rotated the duty of taking minutes of the meetings, so the notes often appeared in laughably different styles. As might be expected, some members of the group had excellent speaking skills but struggled to put their thoughts down on paper.

Agendas always called first for approving the minutes of the previous meeting. At this particular session, the previous notetaker had meant to say that some workers expressed anger that various parties did not show proper appreciation for the work that they were doing. It was easily said, but not so easily written. The garbled minutes merely said the workers wanted a party.

The men and women at this current meeting already remembered that previous discussion and knew quite well the context of the remark. But they spontaneously burst into laughter and competed with each other to suggest amenities for the "party" that the notetaker unwittingly called for. "Should we have balloons?" one asked. "I think we should serve cake," said another. "Yes, let them eat cake," a third agreed.

The hilarity over the party continued for five minutes. But finally, Gretchen fell silent and folded her hands on the table in front of her. Everyone recognized this as her signal for attention, more powerful than if she has shouted at them to quiet down. The entire group stopped talking almost at once, and also folded their hands on the table.

* * *

Gretchen's twelfth birthday was approaching, so her catechism classes took on a sense of urgency. She must study hard to prepare herself to receive her First Communion. Her parents had told aunts and uncles to mark their calendars for that special day, so the girl must not disappoint them.

Today, the priest himself had come to visit with her class to give them encouragement. After the children listened to a reading from the Gospels, Father Graham asked them if they had any questions. Gretchen raised her hand.

"Father, I know some of his enemies called Jesus a glutton because they always heard so many stories about him eating with other people. But it is true. So many of these stories are about him having meals with other people. His enemies and his friends. Why is that?"

The priest nodded. "That is an excellent question, young lady. Yes, why are there so many stories about him eating? This is very important. In those days there were very strict rules about whom you could eat with. The rich would not want to have been seen eating with the poor. The very pious people would not eat with sinners. And if somebody had touched a dead body or done any of a number of things that would make them ritually unclean—well then, nobody at all would share a meal with them," Father Graham said.

"But the remarkable thing about Jesus was that he would sit down at the table and share a meal with anyone who wanted to talk to him about God the Father. It did not matter if you were rich or poor, a sinner or a saint. Jesus would share a meal with you and make you feel accepted into the human family."

Father Graham turned to look at Gretchen directly. "And why do you think he did this, young lady?"

Young Gretchen thought of the many family dinner events where the adults had argued with each other about things she did not understand. Some of the arguments got to the stage of them shouting at each other. But when the meal started, they would bow their heads in prayer and be friends again.

"Father, I think something magic happens when people share a meal together."

The priest beamed. "Young lady, that is absolutely correct. You have taught your entire class an important lesson today."

* * *

After the crew leaders and shop stewards had quieted themselves and turned to Gretchen expectantly, she looked each of them in the eye in silence. After making eye contact with each person seated around the table, she spoke.

"If we were to have a party, where would we hold it?" Gretchen asked.

The others looked left and right at each other. "You mean a real party, boss?" one asked.

"Yes, a party to congratulate our workers on a job well done. I think they deserve it," she replied.

Melissa, sitting next to Gretchen, said, "We have hundreds of workers. We would need someplace big."

Bill, across the table, said in a matter-of-fact voice, "We should hold it on a union hall."

"That would take a lot of balls," Gretchen laughed, "especially after that confrontation your crew had not long ago."

"That's exactly why I would want it at a union hall," Bill replied quickly. "I want our workers to be proud of their organization, and what better way than to have a party in another union's home. In fact, I think it would be fun to invite some of the city's public works people to join the fun. Instead of yelling at each other, let's hoist a beer together."

That was how it started. After calling around, Gretchen settled on a very large union hall not far from Fisherman's Wharf. The building had a circular shape and—especially attractive—had its own parking lot as well as proximity to public transit lines, making attendance more convenient. About one hundred and fifty of the cleanup workers arrived at the door at or shortly after opening time.

Surprisingly, nearly a hundred city workers showed up as well. When Gretchen saw them with their city union shoulder patches, she feared for the worst, that a brawl would break out. But the prospect of free food and drink appeared to melt whatever hostilities they might have harbored. As Gretchen walked through the hall, with recorded music playing loudly enough for background noise but quietly enough to allow for conversation, she saw the two groups mixing freely and laughing at each other's jokes and tales of their supervisors' impossible demands. No matter what line of work or what company people worked for, stories about their unreasonable and demanding supervisors always crossed all lines of division.

Now, outside in the parking lot to talk to her new contact, she had reason to hope for the best. This talk had the potential for disaster, but a wave of optimism warmed her breast as she approached the man standing near an overhead light. After all, when people share food and drink together, magic happens.

"Ms. Vandella, Larry Johnson, head of the labor council," the man said, extending his hand. She grasped his hand and shook warmly.

"Mr. Johnson. Please call me Gretchen, and I will call you Larry. I am so tired of Mr. This and Ms. That. I need to talk to real people once in a while."

He chuckled. "I knew I liked you for some reason. Listen, I asked you out here to thank you for what you and your crew have done here tonight. Our people haven't had cause to celebrate in a mighty long time. I certainly didn't expect them to celebrate with your group, considering they had been led to believe you were taking away their jobs."

Inwardly, Gretchen felt a great relief. She had not realized how much pent-up anxiety she had been holding in the buildup to this conversation, until it all suddenly dissipated.

"Larry, I am not a church-going woman very much these days, but I remember something a wise priest told me when I was younger. He said the most important thing Jesus did was not the miracles but sitting down to eat and drink with people from all walks of life, including his enemies. Something magic happens when people share a meal. It was something that just wasn't done in those days in that culture, and that was what made him stand out."

"Well," Larry said, "you learned the lesson well, and you certainly stand out in this city now. I asked to talk to you out here to ask if you would mind if I nominate you to join the labor council and represent the union your workers created on their own."

Gretchen smiled but shook her head, holding her palms forward to signal a stop. "I am not the union. I am not one of the workers. I am management, remember? But I will introduce you to the head of our workers' union, and I am sure he would be happy to work with you."

"That would be fine." Larry changed his tone to one more personal. "And now I am going to take a risk. I learned many years ago never to ask a woman when she is due to give birth, because there is the possibility that she is not pregnant. Then she will think you are just calling her fat.

And the conversation will never recover after that. But I have seen plenty of pictures of you taken in just the past few months, so I think I am safe in asking. Is this bump that's showing on you something new?"

She placed her hands against her stomach. "Yeah, this is new for me. Scary as hell, but I think I am going to like being a mom."

Larry whistled. "Yeah. Whether it is a girl or a boy, that kid is going to grow up knowing how to kick some ass. Maybe I should wait a few more months and nominate your baby to join the council."

38

CHAPTER 38

Eighteen-year-old Gretchen closed her locker and spun the combination knob to ensure that it remained locked. Clasping her textbook and iPad to her breast, she turned and navigated her way between other students rushing to their next class. As the end of the spring semester approached and the summer break beckoned, many students were putting extra effort into their studying to guarantee decent grades. Nobody wanted to be forced to go to summer school to make up incomplete or failed courses.

A pair of freshmen boys ran past her, laughing almost like children playing tag. Gretchen guessed that they had either pulled a prank on a friend or, worse yet, goosed a girl from behind and were speeding to avoid getting caught. Go ahead, you fools, she thought to herself. When an upper classman intentionally trips you as you're running past and you land on your face in a crowded hallway, or you pinch a girl who is going to fight back and bop you in the balls, you will learn a lesson that you won't soon forget. Like a child who has barely grown tall enough to see the top of the kitchen stove, you might have to burn your fingers before you learn to keep your hands away from the flames.

Turning a corner, Gretchen almost collided with a familiar figure. "Miss Granger! I haven't seen you for weeks. How have you been?"

The gym teacher smiled grimly. "I have been using up some vacation days I still had on the books," she said. "I am going to be retiring at the end of this semester."

"Retiring? But you look way too young for that," Gretchen said, keeping her voice down so other students would not hear. "Seriously, I thought you were at least 20 years away from retirement age.

This time, Miss Granger's smile looked warm and genuine. "Thank you, my dear. That means a lot coming from a beauty like you. But I am not stopping work. I am just leaving this school district. I have enough years on the job in this district that I will be able to collect a pension when I reach the age. But I need to move on."

Gretchen nodded at the logic behind the pension but pressed on. "I can understand that, but why leave? Were you unhappy here? Was there some other line of work that you wanted to pursue?"

The teacher started to speak but stopped herself. Taking Gretchen's elbow, she moved the younger woman away from the flow of foot traffic and out of earshot of any passing students. Before speaking again, she glanced first over her left shoulder and then her right. She spoke in a low voice.

"Do you remember when I hit that boy who was attacking you?"

"Yes, the four boys who attacked me outside the school dance. You saved me. At the time, I actually hoped you would use that baseball bat to bash all four of them."

The gym teacher averted her eyes downward. "Yes, that is how I felt at the time too. But the boy's parents accused me of assault with a deadly weapon, and they filed a lawsuit against the school district. The case has been kept quiet these two years while the attorneys negotiated a settlement. The district will only have to pay a relatively small amount of money—compared to what they expected to have to shell out, anyway, though it still seems a huge amount to me—but one of the terms of the agreement is that I can no longer teach here."

Gretchen stood stock still as she absorbed the information. "He attacked me. He committed a crime. But you are losing your job for stopping the crime and protecting me?"

Miss Granger nodded. "Yep. That's about the size of it."

"But that's not right. It is not fair," Gretchen protested. "It makes no sense."

The teacher placed her hand on the younger woman's arm. "Gretchen, one lesson you will learn as you grow older is that common sense does not always dictate what otherwise intelligent people and organizations will actually do. In this case, they said swinging the baseball bat was using excessive force, that I could have just ordered the four boys to stop by using the authority of my voice and my position as a teacher. And the district's legal department made the decision that the cost of going to court would be much higher than just paying the settlement to make it go away. That is how a lot of lawsuits end up—they are settled before ever going to court."

The young woman still could not grasp what she was hearing. "But I was the one who was attacked. How come I never heard anything about all of this in the past two years?"

"Gretchen," the teacher said, "you were not a party to the lawsuit. This was just between the school district and the boy's parents. Under order from the school district's attorney, I was not allowed to say a word about it while the litigation was still pending. But the settlement is signed and executed now, so it is over. All that is left is for me to finish the semester. The teacher's union was able to get me enough time on the job to finish the school year, so that I would qualify for my pension. I am grateful for that."

The one-minute warning bell rang to let students know the next period was about to start. "You said the agreement is signed and executed, so the litigation is no longer pending?" Gretchen asked.

"That's right. It's over now.'

"Then that means there is no longer a gag order on discussing it?"

Miss Granger's eyes pleaded silently. "Gretchen, I want to leave here quietly. Don't say anything to anybody about my involvement in this matter, please. Can I count on you to help me avoid any legal complications?"

"Absolutely," Gretchen answered. "Your name stays out of it. But I might decide later that I want to go after the four boys who did it. Mr.

Beck frightened me into silence before, saying my own reputation would be ruined if I said anything but that nothing would happen to the boys. If I do not mention your name so that it won't hurt you personally, I might want to say something later. And I don't care what it does to the school district."

The teacher gave Gretchen's arm a squeeze. "My paperwork is completed already, so I am safe. You do what you think you need to do."

39

Women she talked to and experts on TV had said so many wonderful things about this process. That she would feel a sense of fulfillment. That she would have a spiritual epiphany, as if connecting a direct link to God. That her bond with Mark would be cast in granite, making their love eternal. That before, during, and after the birth, she would be one with her child.

They lied.

Yes, Mark was in the room. Between the most intense periods of pain, he would get her up and walk her around a bit. And when the contractions started again, he would hold her hand and remind her to breathe. He would tell her that she was doing great and that he loved her. When her own body told her it was time to push, he would dutifully shout, "Push!" as if she needed to be told. Then, after the pushing produced no results and she had to sit back again in exhaustion, he would lovingly coo words of encouragement and wipe the sweat off her face with a napkin. Yes, Mark was doing all the things the experts said that he should do.

But the pain! She felt no bond to Mark at this moment. *He* wasn't feeling any pain! She felt no eternal bond to the baby, whether it was a boy or girl. As near as she could tell, the baby wasn't feeling any pain either. No, it was only Gretchen herself. *She* was bearing all the pain for Mark, who after all was the one who caused this condition in the first place. If he dared to say even one more time that he knew how she felt, she would leap off the delivery table and strangle him.

"There, there, baby, everything is going to be all right." There he went again! He had said this so many times before. Gretchen knew that within moments, he would start in on how he knew how she—

"Aaaaaaahhhhh!" The scream erupted from her throat of its own accord. It was not her body telling her to push this time. *It was the baby.* Hey, whoever is in charge out there, I want out. It is time to push, dammit! You only have one task, lady, so get yourself in gear and do your job. Push! I want out, and I need you to do your job!

Obedient to the stronger will emanating from her womb, Gretchen pushed hard. Inhaling a deep gulf of breath into her lungs, she pushed down again. Something seemed to be changing. Inhaling a lungful of air to exhale during the exertion again, she gave another push, as hard as she could.

Something seemed to pop. The pressure wasn't completely gone, but it seemed different now.

"I can see the baby's head," cried the nurse. "You are almost done, my dear. Push again."

"Yes, push!" Mark said, still holding her hand. As she prepared to push again, one corner of her mind pictured Mark finally releasing her hand, and then she would jump up at him and wrap all ten of her fingers around his throat. She would be unable to strangle with only one hand— she needed him to release his grip on the one he was holding. But the rest of her mind commanded her full focus, and she obediently pushed.

And then it was out! Gretchen heard a baby wail, and the nurse cooing gently. Mark clenched Gretchen's hand even tighter than before. The nurse wrapped the baby in a light cloth and smiled broadly. "Mama, let me introduce you to your new daughter. Do you know what you will name her?"

Gretchen had thought about this, but she kept it from Mark. She suspected that Mark was secretly hoping for a son and had probably spent time pondering boys' names. He had not shared his ideas with her, so she felt justified not sharing hers with him. They had deliberately declined to ask her doctor what the unborn baby's gender was.

"Laurel. She shall be called Laurel."

The nurse beamed. "Laurel. What a lovely name. Well, Laurel, let me introduce you to your mama. That is what you will call her from now on. Mama." With that, she passed the baby to Gretchen's outstretched arms. And the new mama gingerly cuddled Laurel against her chest. Instinctively, she began cooing in fluent baby talk. And she felt quite certain that Laurel understood every word of it.

Mark lightly touched the back of his finger to the baby's cheek. "Hello, Laurel. I am your papa. But don't worry about me. Mama is more important."

Then, looking into Gretchen's eyes, he asked, "Is Laurel named for the evergreen, or for the little crown?"

"Both. She is going to be as shiny as the laurel leaf. And she is a symbol of victory. And Mark," she added, leveling her eyes at his, "this little girl is going to kick ass. So just remember not to get in her way."

He held up his hands as if she were pointing a gun at his chest. "I would never dream of it. Her mother has taught me well. I know my place in the order of the universe, and I will stay in my place."

40

While the rest of the ambassadors oohed and aahed in a circle around the baby carrier sitting on a desk in the middle of the room, Gretchen gave files and instructions on how to handle each of them to Candy, Heidi and Melanie. who would be taking over her caseload during her maternity leave from the agency. Even though she was now vice president, Gretchen had insisted on maintaining a partial caseload so that she could stay close to what her staff was experiencing in the field.

Candy would also continue to fill in part-time for day-to-day routine duties downstairs at The City That Knows How but would call Gretchen at home for all major decisions. When they discussed it earlier between themselves, Candy had asked, "Are you sure? You will have enough on your hands with the baby. Do you really want me to call you too?"

"Absolutely," Gretchen said. "I have met many women who spent their entire maternity period talking only to their babies. When they came back to their regular lives in the outside world, they had forgotten how to speak to adults. All they could do was baby talk. Goo goo, gaa gaa. Not me."

So now, as they huddled around the desk in her Aurora cubicle, Gretchen tried to funnel the more difficult files to Heidi and Melanie so that Candy would have more time to also deal with TCTKH. As she distributed the individual files, she wrote a list of which was being assigned to whom so she could keep Eric informed.

Laurel squealed from the middle of the room and began crying. "Hey, Mommy, you have been summoned. The boss of the Fischer household has spoken." called out Stephanie.

Gretchen walked to the desk in the middle of the room and lifted Laurel out of the baby carrier. She held the tiny girl against her chest in the crook of her arm. "Hello, Laurel, have you been teaching all these beautiful women what they have to do to serve you properly?" The baby cried again. "Oh, you are hungry, are you?"

Gretchen sat in the chair in the far corner of the office and opened her blouse. She moved Laurel's face toward her breast, and the baby greedily put her lips over the nipple and began sucking.

As the ambassadors began cooing in baby talk, Eric caught Rick's eye and signaled for him to take a photo. Rick discreetly pulled his cell phone from his pocket and took pictures from a number of angles. All the ambassadors kept their eyes on the mother and baby, so no one noticed Rick was shooting dozens of pictures of the scene from in between the ambassadors, from behind, from both sides, and while standing on a chair above and behind them.

When the baby had finished her meal, Gretchen tucked her breast back inside her blouse. Laurel gurgled contentedly and then closed her eyes. She leaned her head against her mother's chest and went to sleep.

Holding their forefingers against their lips to signal for silence, the women dispersed to their own cubicles to get back to work. Eric caught Gretchen's eye and motioned toward his office. Gretchen carried Laurel in her arms as she entered and took a seat.

"Baby Girl." Eric started in a soft voice but caught himself before continuing. "Well, I guess I can't call you Baby Girl anymore. That title has been taken by the little one there."

"Boss, I will always be your Baby Girl."

Eric nodded with a grin. "Gretchen, I want you to take as much time as you need. Little Laurel is more important than the day-to-day stuff here at the office. And I wanted to thank you for giving us the account for The City That Knows How. I promise you that we will take good care of it."

"Of course, you will," she said in a low, soothing voice that would not jar the baby awake. "I trust you implicitly, and Candy will deal with any issues that come up administratively. But most of the work on the streets will be handled by the workers' crew leaders. So, Candy should not need more than five to ten hours a week."

Eric raised one hand from his desk in a salute. "I can't believe how well you have groomed Candy. As you probably guessed a long time ago, I mostly hired her for the photo shoots. I never gave her any speaking parts."

"You are not the only man who has underestimated women. And if a woman has a beautiful face and figure, men almost automatically write her off as an airhead. You should know that better than anyone."

"Guilty as charged," he admitted. "Anyway, before you take off for the next several months, I wanted to ask your permission to use one more image of you. I am not even sure which campaign we would use it for, but I wanted to check if it would be okay when the time comes."

She snorted but covered her mouth with her free hand as Laurel stirred. "Eric, whether you call me vice president, ambassador, or clerical assistant, I am still an employee of the Aurora Marketing Agency. I signed a contract that gives you the authority to use my image in any way that you see fit. You don't need to ask for my permission."

"Yeah, I know," he said. "But the picture might include someone who did not sign a contract. That's why I asked."

Eric dialed a number on his phone. "Rick, could you come into my office? And the baby is sleeping, so keep quiet or else her mother will kick your ass. And then I will too. And when Baby Laurel gets old enough, she will probably kick your ass too if you disturb her sleep."

Several minutes later, Heidi happened to glance through the window of Eric's office. The door was closed, but she could see Eric, Gretchen, and Rick leaning over the desk, scrutinizing the screen on a smart phone.

41

CHAPTER 41

Eighteen-year-old Gretchen nodded to herself with satisfaction as she assessed the scene before her. The bleachers were slowly filling up with parents, grandparents and even a number of freshmen, sophomores, and juniors here to support the graduates. The weather had cooperated, providing a warm evening with clear skies—no hint of rain in the air or forecast. Just as she had hoped, the speaker's platform was erected in the middle of the football field, with ample space on the grass in front of it to accommodate Gretchen's plans.

Recalling the details of her plan, Gretchen scrutinized the growing crowd more closely. She did not see any young children accompanying the adults to their seats. Good, she thought to herself. Let's hope it stays that way. The subject matter might not be suited to young children's ears.

She clutched her flat notebook against her chest. It contained her speech printed out in large letters, lines double spaced, so that she would have no problem reading it at the podium. But Gretchen had read the speech out loud to herself and in front of the mirror so many times that she was certain that she had memorized every word. When writing the first draft, the words had flowed fluently and effortlessly from her mind to her fingers, from the keyboard to the computer screen. She had printed it out, left it alone for a few days, and then came back to read it again with fresh eyes and make any needed corrections. In the past three weeks, she had repeated that process four times, so that she felt confident she had boosted the most important points and minimalized or deleted the unnecessary chaff.

Finally, she had read the final draft to her mother. This scared her more than facing the five hundred people who would be sitting in the stands tonight and the more than three hundred graduating seniors who would be seated on the football field. If her mother disapproved of the speech, she would either have to argue her case passionately, or give the speech as it was written anyway and risk her mother's wrath afterward, or abandon the text of the draft completely and write some vanilla remarks that would cause no offense. The third choice sickened her, and she would not want to even speak if she could not say anything of substance. The second choice also caused a wrenching of her stomach, because her mom was her closest friend, and she did not want to directly disobey her. It would cause an irreversible shift in their relationship, and she did not want to live the rest of her life at odds with her mom and lacking her complete trust and support.

The first choice frightened her also. Though Gretchen would argue passionately if her mother found the speech offensive, she did not want to be forced into that position. For one thing, it would mean that she and her mother did not agree on this major point. Realizing that there was such a difference between them in their thinking would probably cause Gretchen to cry during the argument, and she did not want to shed tears in front of her mother in an argument. Not at this stage of her life, as she was stepping into adulthood. Not now, when she was graduating at the top of her class and wanted to make her mark as a mature leader. Not now, when she needed the support of the most important person in her life, her mom.

Gretchen had waited until the previous afternoon. Her mother had come home from the lunch shift for a few hours and did not have to return to the restaurant until five o'clock for the dinner rush. At four in the afternoon, Gretchen asked her mom to sit comfortably in the living room so she could run through her speech. The older woman took a seat in the middle of the sofa, a cup of fresh coffee on the table in front of her.

Though so much hung on this reading, though she had so much trepidation about whether her mother would approve, Gretchen nevertheless read it in a confident voice, giving proper emphasis to the right phrases, and making eye contact at peak moments. She gave dramatic pauses at the moments that she had planned dramatic pauses. She softened her voice at the appropriate moments, and she almost shouted at the moments that the text of her remarks called for it. This would be the most important performance that she had given in her life up to this point, and she poured every bit of skill, intellect, and emotion into it that she had in her soul.

Afterward, her mother stood, approached Gretchen, and wrapped her arms around her in a tight hug.

"Baby, I have never told you what it is like for me waiting tables every night. When I am leaning over to put a dish in front of a diner, a man at the table might push his face forward to nuzzle one of my boobs through my blouse. Or he might reach up under my skirt to put his fingers on my ass and give a pinch, or worse. I depend on tips, so I have to mostly just smile and put up with it or else we would never have enough to pay the bills. But that does not mean I have ever liked it."

Her mom held Gretchen out at arm's length and looked deeply into her eyes. "I have always been proud of you. I was prouder still when you won all those awards at school, and when you won several scholarships to pay your way through the university. But Baby, I have never been prouder of you than at this very moment. Stay here for a moment. I have a few things I want to show you."

Her mother left the room. Though she had told herself she did not want to cry during this exchange with her mom, the tears flowed freely down Gretchen's cheeks. But these were not tears of anger, frustration, or disappointment. These tears came from the joy of knowing that she had fulfilled something that Father Graham had told her sternly at her first communion when she was just twelve years old. "Jesus said the law could be summed up in two commandments. Love God with all your heart, with all your mind, and with all your soul. And love your neighbor as yourself," the priest said. "But I think I can summarize even those two with the Fifth Commandment. Honor your father and your mother.

That does not necessarily mean to just obey them. Bring honor to them with everything you do. If you follow the two commands Jesus gave you, and you act with such integrity in everything that you do that you bring honor to your family and its name, then you will have done what God has asked."

And now, more than a dozen years later, Gretchen felt that she had finally done what Father Graham instructed her to do.

Gretchen's mother reentered the room and stood before her, hands clasped secretively behind her back.

"Baby, I was going to wait until graduation night to give you this. But I am so proud of the speech you have written that I want to share this with you now. And there is one other spot in your speech that I especially want you to emphasize, but I'll show you that in a few minutes. First, there is this."

The woman brought one of her hands from behind her back and held it out. She held a fob with a pair of keys dangling from it. "Baby, you should ordinarily get to pick out your first car, but I wanted this to be a surprise. I did not buy you a luxury model or a convertible, but it is safe, good quality, and economical enough for you to use it at your university without worrying about having enough money for gas or maintenance."

Gretchen shrieked in shock and surprise. "Mom, how on earth were you ever able to afford this? I can't accept it," she exclaimed, shaking her head from left to right vehemently. "No, I can't push you into debt like this. I will get a part-time job to support myself through school. I won't make you suffer."

Her mother smiled but held one finger to her lips. "I will not suffer. I have been planning and saving for this for many years, longer than you can imagine. And that brings me to the second thing I wanted to show you."

She brought her other hand out from behind her back. In it, she held a small, thin folded passbook. "This will be yours, baby, to put yourself through school and get yourself started in your career, whatever that may be."

Gretchen took it from her mother and looked inside. It was the passbook for a savings account. Gretchen gasped as she slowly leafed through the pages of deposits dating back years. The first deposit had been made on her fourth birthday and was followed by sizable deposits every three months for the past fourteen years. When Gretchen reached the final page and saw the current balance in the account, her entire body shook with sobs.

"Mom, how on earth did you do this?"

Her mother grinned. "I told you that a lot of men put their hands on me when I was waiting their tables? Yeah, well I put up with it, and they left me tips on the table that went way beyond the eighteen or twenty percent that is fashionable these days. In fact, sometimes they left as much as their entire dinner and bar tab. Now, before you ask," she said, in reaction to the worried look on Gretchen's face, "no, I never let a single one of these men sleep with me. But they all had wives who came to the restaurant with them occasionally, and I kept the men's secrets. If they were so fascinated with my face, boobs, and butt, then I was going to use that against them. I took their money, and lots of it."

She grinned. "And Baby, I not only saved a lot for you, but I put away a lot more for myself too. While you are away at the university, I am going to quit my job and open my own restaurant. Later this weekend, after graduation, I will take you to show you the location I have selected. I am going to hire women who have been grabbed and groped ever since they hit puberty, and I am going to help them use their brains, beauty, and bodies to gain independence. And that brings me back to your speech. Set it out on the coffee table her."

She and Gretchen pored over a few paragraphs in the text, the mother pointing to a spot and saying, "Here. And there too."

After Gretchen had added the few lines to the text in scribbled ink, the two of them got up from the couch and faced each other. Mother and daughter laughed and cried, and their bodies shook as they stood clutching each other.

And tonight, Gretchen looked up from the football field and could see her mother sitting squarely in the middle of the bleachers, right on the fifty-yard line, midway up so that she would be high enough to see all that happened but not so far back that the crowd would block her view. They waved to each other and then Gretchen took her seat with the other graduating seniors.

School administrators and officials from the school district sat in a separate block of chairs to the left side of the stage. When each senior's name was called, that student would pass by the administrators' seats, climb the stairs to where the podium stood in the center of the small stage, accept their diploma, and exit via another set of stairs on the right side of the stage.

Mrs. Gallagher, the principal, climbed to the podium to call the ceremony to order. After the usual welcoming remarks, she introduced Gretchen as the class valedictorian and invited her to the stage to give her remarks. Mrs. Gallagher came down the stairs and met Gretchen on the grass of the football field to shake the young woman's hand, and then the principal took her seat with the other administrators. Gretchen took the stage alone and stood behind the podium. She opened the notebook and set the speech text out where she would be able to see it.

"Graduating class of Parker High School, let's give ourselves a hand. We made it!" The students and adults in attendance all applauded loud and long.

"Several people told me that, in my speech, I should exhort you to end hunger, solve homelessness, put an end to all wars, and promote peace and brotherhood throughout the world." She looked up at the crowd and held out her arms to both sides. "Okay, go do those things. But that still leaves me another ten or fifteen minutes that I am supposed to fill with words up here, so I'll add a bit more."

Laughter erupted from the bleachers but quickly subsided.

"All of our graduates tonight deserve high praise for their accomplishments, but I especially want to give attention to the women because they never get as much recognition as they deserve. First, can all the members of the Girls Scholastic Club please come forward and stand over here," Gretchen said, pointing to the grassy area at the bottom of the steps to the right side of the stage. As the girls stood up from their seats both among the seniors and the sophomores and juniors in the bleachers, the rustling of movement raised the noise level briefly.

"And now, could the members of the girls' track, volleyball, basketball, and softball teams please gather over here." Gretchen pointed to the area between the base of the steps and the administrators' block of seats. After more rustling of chairs and many voices saying, "Excuse me, excuse me," as the ladies edged their way out of their rows of chairs, a large group of girls congregated on the grass in the area to the front and left of the stage.

Now Gretchen got to the section her mother had suggested the day before. Gretchen put a lot of feeling into her voice now. "And finally, I want to give recognition to some women who get plenty of public admiration for their beauty and physical abilities, but almost never for their intellectual prowess. And believe me, these women are smart too. Most people just never think to speak to them and find how really smart they are. Could I please have the women of the cheerleading squad here in the middle."

This brought cheers from the men but also loud whoops of joy from the women, especially from the cheerleaders themselves. They lined up on the grass in front of center stage. Then, as if they had rehearsed it, they performed a quick routine of dancing, kicking up their legs, jumping and shouting praises to Parker High.

"Ladies and gentlemen," Gretchen said into the microphone, "I could not call up every single woman in the graduating class and the rest of the school who so richly deserves your attention, but these women before you now represent all the others. Let's give the women of Parker High a rousing round of applause."

The crowd rose for a standing ovation. The clapping and cheering went on for more than half a minute, at which point Gretchen motioned for the crowd to sit down.

Gretchen put a serious tone into her voice.

"I was told that, as valedictorian, I represent every student in our graduating class. But all these young women in front of you have had to overcome the same type of obstacle, and I represent them on that count as well. I want to tell you a story, a true story. It happened to me, but it represents something that has happened in one way or another to every girl in this school, and not this school alone."

Now that the moment had come, Gretchen felt a knot in the pit of her stomach. This could well bring her hoped-for career to an end before it even started if things did not turn out well. So much was riding on mixing just the right amount of emotion into her voice. Too much would sound like defenseless whining; not enough would sound cold and dispassionate.

"More than two years ago, four boys sexually assaulted me here at the school. They conspired to lure me into a secluded place where no one would hear me struggling, and then they all set upon me physically at the same time."

Many people in the crowd gasped, and a buzz of conversation arose from the bleachers.

"Fortunately," Gretchen continued, raising her voice a bit louder to drown out the noises of the crowd, "a teacher intervened forcefully and stopped them before they were able to go through with their plan to actually gang-rape me. That teacher had to physically strike two of the boys to make them and the others stop."

Gretchen paused for a moment. "But the school administration—a male administrator, I should point out—advised me to not report the incident to the police, because little or nothing would be done to the boys. But *I* would be labeled a slut. He told me that *my* reputation would be damaged, but nothing would happen to the boys. So, I remained silent. But the parents one of the boys who the teacher hit sued the school district for what they called an attack with a deadly weapon. That's right, one of the boys who assaulted me claimed that he was the victim. He and the other boys got off scot-free, the school district was forced to pay a settlement in the lawsuit, and I was forced to remain silent about the violence they had done against me."

At this point, Mr. Beck and several other administrators and school district officials tried to force their way onto the stage so they could stop Gretchen from saying more. But the young women in front and to the sides of the stage locked their arms together and blocked them from getting to the stairs.

Gretchen continued unabated. "Every day of every week of every month, of every year going back to the beginning of civilization, women have had to take abuse in silence and have had to struggle to get the recognition they deserve for their accomplishments. The women you see before me here tonight have had the same things done to them. The athletes are constantly told their achievements are not as valuable as those of the boys on the male sports teams. The girls who win scholastic honors are told they should concentrate on finding husbands instead of reaching their full potential in their careers. And even those women who devote their lives to raising a family are relegated to second class and taken for granted."

By now, Gretchen was almost shouting. She stood back from the podium to avoid the distortion that would come over the public announcement system if she shouted too closely into the microphone.

"But no more," she stated firmly. "Yes, I represent the graduating class of Parker High when I tell you that *our generation* says it is time to put a stop to this."

Gretchen paused while the young women shouted, "Our generation," three times.

"*Our generation* is going to give equal value to our men and women." Again, Gretchen stopped while the women on the field chanted, "Our generation" again. This time they were joined by all the young women in the senior block of seats and the freshmen, sophomores, and juniors in the bleachers. And they did not stop chanting after just three times. Gretchen finally had to motion for silence.

"*Our generation* will not give less recognition to our men, but we will give just as much to our women. *Our generation* will not make victims of abuse suffer in silence.

"So," Gretchen concluded, "graduating class of Parker High, I salute every one of you. Now let's go out from here as the adults we are meant to be. And let's go kick some ass. Thank you, and good night."

Gretchen stepped away from the podium and walked to the steps at the right of the stage, away from where the administrators were trying unsuccessfully to get to the stage. The entire senior class stood up from their seats and surged to the foot of the stairs of the right, both to hug and cheer for Gretchen as she joined them on the field, but also to shield her from the authorities. When the seniors went back to their seats, they stood and blocked Mr. Beck twice when he tried to approach Gretchen. And when her name was called to come up to the stage to receive her diploma, the entire cheerleading squad accompanied her to the stairs to block the administrators from approaching her. Meanwhile, all the students on the field and in the bleachers continued chanting. "Our generation. Our generation. Our generation."

Gretchen received her diploma and went home with her mother. She never returned to Parker High again.

42

∽

CHAPTER 42

"Would you like me to put her in the crib in the dining room so you can have her near while you eat your lunch with Mr. Fischer?"

"No. Thank you, Barbara, but I think she is getting used to being on her own for brief periods. It is my understanding that it is important for the baby to learn early that she does not get instant attention every time she cries, that she has to slowly learn to become independent. We have the baby monitor broadcasting if she sounds distressed. I think she can rest peacefully while we eat."

"Yes, ma'am. I will just look in on her before I serve your food."

Gretchen still had difficulty adjusting to the idea of having a staff of household workers. Becoming the wife of a billionaire had certainly changed her lifestyle, but she refused to treat the workers like servants. They handled the housecleaning, laundry, and gardening. But the woman of the house, Gretchen, insisted on answering the phone as often as she could, sorting the mail, rinsing her own dishes and loading them in the dishwashing machine, and other small chores. Though Barbara helped keep an eye on Laurel, Gretchen kept most of the motherly duties to herself. And now that the baby had reached her tenth month, her mother was attempting to lessen her hovering over her as Laurel began to explore the world around her. Just last month, she had said, "Mama," for the first time, and a day later, "Papa," when Mark was holding her. While

Gretchen wanted to help her daughter learn, she also wanted the girl to develop her own sense of curiosity and independence.

Gretchen walked into the breakfast nook adjacent to the main dining room and sat at the small, round table that could seat four people. Gretchen did not care for eating a simple meal with Mark at the long formal table in the main dining room. She reserved that one for dinner parties and meetings. Even during her maternity leave, she often met with local business and labor leaders, and the occasional politician. It seemed so cartoonish for just Mark and herself to eat a small meal at one end of a table with twenty-two empty chairs. And sitting across from each other in the middle of the table only made it seem worse, to her way of thinking.

Mark entered the breakfast nook speaking on his cell phone and sat at the table in the chair next to Gretchen. She caught his eye, pointed at her ear, and then wagged her finger back and forth before pointing at the surface of the table.

"I am sorry, Mitch. I have to get off the phone. Can I get back to you in about an hour?" After a moment's pause, he said thanks and hung up. As Gretchen had insisted since that day that she moved into this mammoth house, he dutifully turned the power on the phone off and put it in his pants pocket while he was at the table to eat a meal with her.

Barbara brought in a tray and placed it on a counter on the side of the room. She lifted two bowls of clam chowder from the tray and placed them in from of Gretchen and Mark. And, in a break from formal tradition that Gretchen had instituted since moving in, Barbara then placed small plates of salad to the left of each of their place settings. Gretchen thought it pretentious to make Barbara serve the first two courses separately when only she and Mark were at the table. Save the formality for special dinners with guests, she had told her.

After Barbara left the room, the couple folded their hands in front of them and bowed their heads for a moment in silence. Between them, they had come to agree that praying aloud sometimes led to disagreements over theological interpretations among other people they had known over the years, and that praying aloud almost always resulted in self-centered begging for a specific outcome in a specific situation. Neither of them felt right telling God what to do, so they prayed in silence.

Mark unfolded his napkin and spread it across one of his upper legs. "Do you want to know who that was on the phone?"

"Not if it is going to spoil my lunch, force me to write a check to some charity, or compel me to have tea with the local PTA when my own child is still years away from kindergarten," Gretchen said dryly as she blew softly to cool off her spoonful of hot soup.

Her husband did not let the snarky reply deter him. "No charities that I am aware of yet, and no PTA meetings. But I do not know if it will spoil your lunch."

"If you are not sure, then maybe you shouldn't say anything."

He smiled. "Ah, that would be the safest route. Take no chances. But hey, I am in the horse racing business. My living depends on people playing the odds and taking chances."

"But the only time you gain is when those people take a chance and lose." She exhaled loudly. "Okay, I can see that you are not going to let up until you tell me who it was. So go ahead, and I hope this gets the Show & Tell urge out of your system."

Mark set down his soup spoon, and he reached across before Gretchen could scoop up more chowder and put his hand over hers, pushing her hand and spoon down onto her placemat. Startled, she looked up and found him gazing directly into her eyes.

"That was Mitch Claymore, a senior representative with the State Department. The United States Ambassador to the United Nations is going to be making an address to the General Assembly next week. The ambassador has asked if you could be present for her speech. She would like to hold you up as an example of what we can achieve by building the economy from the bottom up instead of the top down."

She looked into his eyes and waited. Finally, she said, "What, no punchline? Every joke is supposed to have a punchline. I have been more than patient. You really need to work on your timing, you know."

"I am not joking. If you say yes, Mitch will send a formal invitation by courier service, along with round-trip airline tickets and a hotel reservation in New York. From what I gather, the ambassador is not asking for you to speak. She only wants you in the gallery with other spectators so that she can ask you to stand up when she makes reference to you in her speech.'

"Oh, my God," Gretchen muttered. "I am so glad I resumed my workouts at the gym and took off the fat I gained when I was pregnant with Laurel. Or maybe I should have Laurel in my arms when I stand up? Oh shit, we have to call and find out if she wants me to wear any particular color. You know, sometimes it is a special occasion, and everybody wears canary yellow or pea green or some obscure shade. Can you call and check for me?"

"Whoa, slow down, cowgirl. Can I take this to mean that yes, you will appear at the United Nations for her speech?"

"Yes, but why on earth did she ask for me?"

"Well, you are an ambassador, after all. But listen, though Mitch did not say it in so many words, I think the ambassador will want you to accompany her to a reception afterwards. She will want to introduce you to some important people."

Gretchen stopped speaking and her eyes glazed over as she did some inward calculations. "Then this part is serious. When we call your friend Mitch back, I will need a list of names and background information on the people she plans to introduce me to. I built my career on knowing in advance as much as possible about people I was going to be working on at meetings and other events. If the ambassador wants me to work a meeting, I need to be prepared as if it were an assignment for Aurora. I need to research their backgrounds, who they work for, what their interests are, and try to figure out what they will be asking me for."

"That's my girl." Mark patted her on the hand and picked up his spoon again. "Now finish your soup before it gets cold."

When Barbara came to retrieve the empty soup bowls, Gretchen asked if the cook had already prepared an entrée. Barbara said no, that because of the delay caused by the couple's lengthy conversation, he had not started it yet. "Then please ask him to save it," Gretchen said. "Or if it is too late to refrigerate it again, maybe you and he can eat it, or anyone else on the staff who hasn't had their lunch yet?"

"I am sure we can find someone," Barbara said, laughing. From the sparkle in her eyes, Gretchen guessed that the woman would love to have the entrée with the cook. Gretchen suspected that the two had a closer relationship than just coworkers.

As they strolled out of the breakfast nook together, Mark took his cellphone out of his pocket and pressed the button to turn on the power. After it booted up, a light on the screen showed him that a voicemail message was waiting for him. He tapped Gretchen's arm and turned on the speaker so both could hear.

"Mark, this is Eric at Aurora. Miss High-and-Mighty apparently can't be bothered to answer my calls or return my messages anymore, so could you please pass this on to her for me? Thanks. Gretchen. Baby Girl. At exactly ten minutes after two, I want you to turn on Channel Eight and sit quietly. I know that sitting quietly doesn't come easily for you these days. And since you are not on the clock and I am not technically your boss right now, I can't order you to sit down and shut up. But as your friend, I am strongly suggesting that you turn on Channel Eight, sit down, and shut up. And Mark, I know that you are only Number Three in the hierarchy of your household there, but could you please exert your influence to make Number Two turn on the TV as I suggested, and sit down and shut up? Thanks for your help."

Mark glanced at his watch. "Hmm, it is almost two o'clock now. I guess we had better turn on Channel Eight. And whatever this is about, I will set the digital recorder to keep a copy of it. It might be important." If he found any offense in Eric telling his wife to sit down and shut up, he showed no signs of it.

Retiring to the den, Mark picked up the remote and turned on the TV. Switching to Channel Eight, he punched in another command and a red dot appeared, which indicated that the show would be recorded. Gretchen started to speak, but he turned sharply and pointed at her.

"You are supposed to be sitting down and shutting up."

She sat down. And did not say anything.

Channel Eight was screening a daytime talk show featuring a panel of female celebrities representing both the right and left wings of political thought. The show was quite popular.

At nine after two, the host of the talk show, herself a huge success and now a mogul in the entertainment industry, looked into the camera and said in a soft voice, "And now, a few words about recent events in San Francisco. As you may have heard, a young woman named Gretchen Vandella has been leading a campaign to clean up the streets and put homeless people to work so they can afford to get a place to live. It has been a fantastic success. As it turns out, Gretchen had a baby and has taken time off to be with her child. But she is still a shining example. We just received this clip from her organization, which calls itself The City That Knows How."

The screen filled with a shot of the Golden Gate Bridge taken from the Marin Headlands looking into the bay, with downtown high-rise buildings visible in the distance. Then it skipped to a video clip of one of her crews steam-cleaning a sidewalk and sweeping garbage from a gutter. A narrator's voice that Gretchen recognized as Candy's said, "San Francisco nourishes our souls. And our workers return the favor, doing what they can to nourish the soul of the city."

Suddenly, the image on the screen switched to a portrait shot of Gretchen taken long before her pregnancy. Gretchen recognized the picture. It was one of the most beautiful shots of her in the agency's archives. Candy's voice over continued, "Gretchen Vandella had a vision. To restore dignity to people who had lost everything. And in so doing, to restore the soul of the city. She has done that, and San Francisco is grateful."

Now the screen was filled with a still shot showing the interior of the Aurora Marketing Agency's office. An overhead view looked down at a circle of more than fifteen women gathered in a semi-circle around a figure sitting in the far corner of the room. The image was replaced by one on the same level as the women, standing slightly behind and peering between their bodies at the figure in the corner. It was now evident that the figure was Gretchen breastfeeding a baby, young Laurel.

Candy's voice continued. "This is The City That Knows How." The image now switched to a closeup of Gretchen with baby Laurel at her breast, and Gretchen looking directly at the camera with a smile and the glow of new motherhood.

"We create life. We nurture life. We help all of us live together with pride and dignity. And we help give life meaning. We are The City That Knows How."

The clip ended with "The City That Knows How" emblazoned across the screen in bold letters.

As the clip ended, the screen reverted to a closeup of the TV talk show's host. She started to speak but choked slightly and caught herself, her eyes glistening with tears. She turned her gaze slightly to the left of the camera and made a cutting motion across her neck with the fingers of one hand. "I can't say anything right now. Please cut to a commercial." Moments later, a familiar pitch for a popular weight-loss pill came on the air, urging viewers to call the toll-free number on the screen or to order directly from the company's website.

Mark turned down the volume on the TV. Gretchen sat in silence, gazing vacantly into the distance. After a few moments, she snapped back into focus and turned to Mark.

"Call your friend, Mitch. I need to know what color dress they want me to wear to the United Nations."

THE END (BUT REALLY JUST THE BEGINNING)

ABOUT THE AUTHOR

Patrick W. Andersen enjoyed a long and successful career as a reporter and editor before turning his talents toward fiction. He is the author of *Second Born* and *Acts of the Women*, two novels about the birth of Christianity. He also published a collection of his short stories, entitled *Moments to Contemplate (In Bite-Sized Servings)*.